A
Harlequin
Romance

WELCOME

TO THE WONDERFUL WORLD

of Harlequin Romances!

Interesting, informative and entertaining,
each Harlequin Romance portrays an appealing
love story. Harlequin Romances take you
to faraway places — places with real people
facing real love situations — and
you become part of their story.

As publishers of Harlequin Romances, we're extremely
proud of our books (we've been publishing
them since 1954). We're proud also that Harlequin
Romances are North America's most-read
paperback romances.

Eight new titles are released every month and are
sold at nearly all book-selling stores across
Canada and the United States.

A free catalogue listing all available Harlequin Romances
can be yours by writing to the

HARLEQUIN READER SERVICE,
M.P.O. Box 707, Niagara Falls, N.Y. 14302.
Canadian address: Stratford, Ontario, Canada.

or use order coupon at back of book.

We sincerely hope you enjoy reading
this Harlequin Romance.

Yours truly,

THE PUBLISHERS
Harlequin Romances

WINDS
FROM THE SEA

by

MARGARET PARGETER

HARLEQUIN BOOKS   TORONTO
WINNIPEG

Harlequin edition published August 1975

SBN 373-01899-1

Original hard cover edition published in 1975
by Mills & Boon Limited.

All the characters in this book have no existence outside the
imagination of the Author, and have no relation whatsoever to
anyone bearing the same name or names. They are not even
distantly inspired by any individual known or unknown to the
Author, and all the incidents are pure invention.

Printed in Canada

1899

CHAPTER ONE

THE car-ferry sailed past Lady's Rock, close under the walls of Duart Castle, and anchored by the pier at Craignure.

Mull at last! Sara heaved a small sigh of relief as she stared around, her blue eyes searching eagerly through the small crowd of people on the pier. James had said that Hugh Fraser would be here to meet her, but she could see no one whom she thought might fit his description. James had sketched him briefly as a big man, in his thirties, tall and dark. She only hoped that having employed her in a hurry, without having seen her, Mr Fraser hadn't just as suddenly forgotten all about her.

With a slight frown creasing her smooth forehead, she turned and gathered up her luggage before scrambling down the narrow gangplank off the boat. The crossing had been choppy, but she had enjoyed it, only it did seem a long time since she'd left Euston yesterday.

Jane, the friend whom she had been staying with in London, had seen her off. "You're bound to have a good journey, darling," she had said cheerfully, after managing to find Sara an almost empty compartment and loading her with magazines.

Sara had travelled overnight to Glasgow, then on by train to Oban, where she had caught the ferry. It had, she supposed, been a good journey, but tiring none the less. Now an urge to reach her destination was uppermost in her mind as she wondered impatiently how long she would have to wait.

Moving a short distance from the boat, Sara dropped her cases haphazardly by her side and gazed curiously across the harbour to Craignure. It seemed a small place, with only a few scattered houses and hotels built almost on the water's edge around the bay. Behind them, in the background, she could see high rugged mountains against the skyline. She noticed that some of the cars from off the ferry were already making their way along the narrow road which, according to her map, led to Tobermory, but there wasn't much sign of life otherwise. Just the sea and the wind and a small boy fishing. A young boy, he seemed, with a bright freckled face, fishing for mackerel while huge white gulls swooped hopefully around.

Intrigued, Sara watched, until a sudden gust of wind caught wildly at one of her smaller bags, rolling it over. Startled, she sprang forward, but before she could reach it someone hurried past her and picked it up. She recognized him almost immediately. She had noticed him earlier on the ferry because he had been whistling an aria from *Rigoletto*. He was thin and young, with a bearded face, and wore tight black velvet trousers with a black sweater. More fitting, she thought, for a Chelsea coffee bar than a Scottish island, but he did grin cheerfully as he returned her bag.

She smiled back quickly. "You were just in time," she said warmly. "Another inch and it would have been over the edge into the water."

"And I can't swim," he joked, laughing as he brushed aside her breathless thanks, his eyes narrowed on her flushed face. "Can I give you a lift anywhere, or are you just deciding where to go?"

Disconcerted, Sara looked away, trying to ignore a

6

faint uneasiness. "We might not be going in the same direction," she murmured, bending to flick an imaginary speck of dust from her anorak. She wished now that she had worn something more conventional than her old blue jeans for travelling in. Obviously this man thought she was just roaming around looking for company. "Actually," she rushed on, not caring for his bold stare, "I'm on my way to Lochgoil to work for Mr Hugh Fraser. I'm to wait for him here, so I really don't need a lift. Thanks all the same."

"Hugh Fraser!" For a moment he looked quite startled, but the impression was so fleeting that afterwards she wasn't sure it had been there at all.

"Oh, well," he shrugged his thin shoulders indifferently, "I'll probably be seeing you." With a careless lift of his hand he turned, and Sara watched silently as he jumped lightly into a shabby old car and drove away.

She stared after him, frowning uncertainly. Had she been too hasty? He had probably only meant to be helpful, but in her present rather overwrought state she found it very easy to jump to the wrong conclusions. Perhaps she shouldn't have been so abrupt, but she didn't want to get involved with another man before Hugh Fraser arrived. She didn't want to start off on the wrong footing, especially as James had intimated that her new boss wasn't an altogether easy man to get on with.

With a sigh she turned away, sitting down on an overturned fish-crate, and prepared to wait. The air smelt of seaweed, fish and salt, and she breathed it deeply, finding the sharpness of it invigorating. She hadn't met Hugh Fraser, not yet. She didn't even know what he looked like apart from what James had told her, and that had been very little.

It seemed strange, and not a little improbable, that

7

she should be sitting here so far from home preparing to start a new job on an island which she had scarcely heard of. Previously it had only been a name on a map, and if it hadn't been for the plane crash which had killed both her parents it might have remained that way.

It was actually Jane who had got her this job. Jane Marlee, who had been a family friend ever since she could remember, and whom Sara had lived with since the accident. Then it had been absolutely necessary that another doctor should take over the house and surgery where her father had practised, and where Sara had been employed as his receptionist. In any case Sara hadn't wanted to live there after her parents had gone.

Jane worked for a well-known firm of solicitors in the West End, and she was personal secretary to James Kerr, one of the senior partners. It was she who had suggested that Sara got right away for a while. She had rung from the office.

"I think you need to, darling," she had said gently. "Much as I hate to part with you, you do need a change. But I haven't been able to think of anything. However, it seems that at last my prayers have been answered in the shape of a Scottish island, and a man called Hugh Fraser."

Into Sara's mystified ear she had poured the rest of her story.

"I don't know this man Fraser, Sara, but James does. Actually he has inherited some property on the island of Mull, and requires someone for about a month or so to help him sort things out. He especially asked James to find him someone who would also be willing to help entertain his young sister—stepsister, I believe. Of course he could probably get one of his own office girls. He's the Fraser bit of Fraser and Harding, the importers. You're sure to have heard of them? Anyway, it seems that he would rather have a stranger, and this is why he rang James."

"But why me?" Sara had interrupted, clutching the receiver tightly in an effort to take in what Jane was telling her.

"Because," Jane had repeated anxiously, "you do need a change, dear, and when James asked if I knew of anyone, I immediately thought of you. We both know how heartbreaking these last few weeks have been, and something like this would be better, I think, than a holiday just now. It would keep you occupied and take your mind off the accident. Anyway, you think about it, and we'll talk it over this evening. If it appeals to you, James will see you in the morning."

Careless of Jane's advice, Sara hadn't thought about it very much. Although it was almost a month since the air-crash her mind still retained a degree of numbness which accepted rather than rationalized. If Jane said that this man Fraser was all right, and that a change of scene would be a good thing, then she was quite willing to co-operate.

Next day she had gone along with Jane to see James Kerr. He was a quiet pleasant man of about fifty, who had been in love with Jane for years. Unfortunately Jane had been divorced, and with one unhappy marriage behind her was unwilling to try matrimony again, but she did go out with him occasionally, and a long time ago had introduced him to Sara's parents, who had liked him very much. Smiling, he waved Sara gently to a chair, pressed the bell for coffee, then told her briefly what would be expected of her. He had seemed quite satisfied with her qualifications, and equally · satisfied that she

9

would suit his client very well.

"I know that Hugh's uncle had a rather elderly retainer who still lives there," he told her as she got up to go. "She's a very efficient cook-housekeeper, so you should be well looked after. Jill, I imagine, could be a bit of a handful, not that I doubt you'll manage very nicely . . ." He had beamed at her reassuringly over the top of his gold-rimmed spectacles.

Jill was the stepsister. Sara stirred restlessly on the fish-crate. She was the reason, James had explained, why Mr Fraser didn't want someone too young, or a middle-aged paragon. Mr Fraser sounded a bit of a paragon himself! Sara hoped, with a quirk of her soft lips, that he would consider her twenty-one-year-old status satisfactory. Over-all Jill didn't appear to constitute much of a problem. All her brother probably had in mind was someone sensible, and agile enough to keep a young girl occupied in an isolated place like this.

She glanced frowning from her wrist-watch to the afternoon sun before the throb of an engine drew her gaze back along the pier. A Land-Rover wheeled off the south road and sped along to the boat. It pulled up with a jerk of brakes and a tall man jumped down. His eyes moved briefly over the rapidly dispersing crowd. He was well but casually dressed in cord trousers and a white crew-necked sweater, clothes that looked well on his hard muscular body. A man who spent most of his time outdoors, Sara guessed. His face had a hard vitality that suggested storm and wind and a liking for dangerous living.

His gaze had reached her now, measured but impersonal. Cool grey eyes surveyed her from under heavy dark brows. She saw the hard curve of his temple and jaw, the sweep of dark hair. He was too tough-looking to be really handsome. Big and interesting, was her final summing up, and almost automatically, because she had been staring, Sara smiled.

His eyes narrowed as his expression changed. The heavy brows lifted slightly and a smile touched his firm mouth, a smile which made Sara's cheeks go pink. It was amused, patronizing, and somehow utterly disconcerting.

He strode over to where she sat, towering above her as he asked sharply, "Do you happen to be Miss Sara Winton, my new secretary?" When Sara nodded awkwardly, her cheeks still pink with confusion, he added smoothly, "I'm Fraser from Lochgoil."

Sara scrambled to her feet. She felt curiously at a disadvantage to have him staring down at her and said with as much dignity as she could muster, "I've only just got off the boat."

"Then perhaps we can get away." Without paying her any more attention he swung her luggage lightly into the back of the Land-Rover, and with a casual wave of his hand indicated that she should climb into the passenger seat.

Sara winced. No use expecting him to open the door. After all, he was her employer. She saw a flicker of amusement on his face as he waited, hands in pockets, while she did as she was told. He could read her thoughts, and the knowledge annoyed her. She supposed the mud-spattered Land-Rover was the best type of vehicle for a Highland estate, but could it not have been tidied out a bit? Fastidiously she surveyed the conglomeration of articles littering the floor. Everything from pickaxes to drainpipes. Her luggage sat regally on top of a bale of straw. She pulled back the hood of her anorak and sat gingerly on the edge of the seat.

"No luxury coach, as you can see." The seat bounced as he settled himself beside her. "Just throw those old papers in the back, and mind that can of engine oil. Had a good journey?"

"Yes . . ." Sara considered his belated inquiry purely conventional. His voice held no real interest.

He reversed carefully off the pier into the road, driving with casual ease, soon leaving Craignure far behind, taking the road north to Salen.

She felt a faint stir of surprise. "You came from the south," she said. The words were out before she could stop them.

"That's right," he replied lazily, with a scarcely discernible lift of dark brows. "I was seeing a man about a dog."

Sara flushed. She was sorry she had spoken. It was, as he implied, none of her business.

"I was, actually." He smiled, glancing with some amusement at her downcast face. "I'm looking for a special breed which is proving difficult to find. This way we go by Salen, then take the road left to Lochgoil. Salen is a small village a few miles up the coast. I could tell you, I suppose, that it was founded by a man called Lachan MacQuarie, a Scotsman who was Governor of New South Wales. When he retired he brought the Salen estate and built the village."

"I see." Sara was not quite sure that she did. Lachan MacQuarie must have been quite a man.

"Been here before?" His voice sharpened.

"No." Her brain could only produce monosyllables.

"If you sat back in your seat you might relax." Patiently he slowed down to allow some sheep to cross the narrow road. The sea at this point was only a few yards away. There was no beach, just shingle which the water lapped gently. Again she did as she was

12

told, and surprisingly found it better. His lips twitched. "We learn to take things easy in this part of the world, although I must admit it takes a bit of getting used to."

He moved forward again as the sheep passed. Sara moistened her bottom lip, watching them go.

"Mr MacQuarie obviously didn't follow that advice," she murmured demurely.

He slanted her a quick look, his eyes glinting. "You're confusing the issue, Miss Winton. Relaxation has nothing whatever to do with laziness."

Already he was proving too sharp for her! She turned her fair head slightly, studying his profile, puzzled, half frowning.

He turned his own head, sensing her prolonged scrutiny.

"What did you expect?" he grinned. "A wild Highlander, complete with a claymore and kilt?"

Colour surged beneath her skin as his mocking eyes met her own. "I hadn't given it a thought," she replied, not quite truthfully.

His gaze left hers, slipping over her tawny loveliness. "Would it be out of line to ask what a girl like you is doing here?"

She wasn't quite sure what he meant. There was an oddly speculative look in his eyes. "You did ask for a secretary," she pointed out.

His eyes touched her pure, averted profile. "I wouldn't have thought a girl with your looks would be keen to work on an island like this, even for a few weeks."

Dismayed, Sara swung around, staring at him defiantly. What was he trying to say? "Perhaps you think I'm too young?" Her pulse gave an apprehensive jerk. Surely he couldn't mean that she was un-

13

suitable? Not when she'd come all this way!

"You misunderstand me." His gaze left her face and swung front again. "I especially asked James Kerr to find me someone youthful. You probably seem too young because I'm older than you are."

James had said he was about thirty-five, not Methuselah! "I can assure you," she said quickly, "that my appearance, one way or another, will in no way interfere with my work." Her words hung on the air, Victorian, starchy. Again Sara's cheeks flamed.

"You sound resentful." He took a packet of cigarettes from his pocket and offered her one. When she shook her head numbly he drew one out for himself, and after lighting it flicked his burnt match through the window.

"Perhaps you should have emphasized plainness when you rang Mr Kerr." Sara stared unhappily out of the window through the haze of smoke from his cigarette.

The road narrowed and suddenly Hugh Fraser whipped the Land-Rover up a side-track and stopped. They were surrounded by dark woods and the smell of Scots pine hung sharply on the thin spring air. Oak, ash, and silver birch stood bare, just coming into leaf, and the wind moaned in the tree-tops accentuating the silence as he switched off the engine.

He looked at her again with easy amusement and that slight lift of black eyebrows which so annoyed her. "I personally have no objection to your being decorative," he smiled. "In case you're wondering, I've stopped because there are things I'd like to discuss before you meet the others."

He considered the glowing end of his cigarette with maddening deliberation, while Sara waited, stirring uneasily, thrusting back her long fair hair with slim nervous fingers. This man repelled and intrigued her, endued her with caution, even after so short a time. There was something about him she couldn't quite make out. He was certainly a bit different from any man she'd ever known. Then, perversely, because she didn't care for mysteries, she asked, "Wouldn't an older woman have suited you better?"

He shifted his weight impatiently in the confining space as he turned towards her inhaling deeply. "Maybe," he said, his eyes on her hair. "But they're not always so adaptable, and often take longer to settle down."

Sara thought she understood. "I suppose you want this job finished as soon as possible?" She smiled politely.

"Not necessarily." His eyes left her hair and studied her face, lazily, like considering a painting. "I did have six weeks in mind, but it would be impossible to give an exact date."

"So we might be finished sooner?"

"Or later. It depends how long I can be here. I might have to spend some time in London. More, I'm afraid, than I thought."

Sara digested this in silence. Of course, she had forgotten. His main business would be in London, not here. She sat for a moment gazing at the dashboard, unaware of his scrutiny. "It mustn't be very convenient living so far away from town," she murmured at last. Then, because it seemed the obvious thing to say, "Jane told me you're an exporter."

"Jane?" Quickly his glance sharpened, his eyes alert.

Sara wished she hadn't said anything. Hastily she tried to explain. "Jane Marlee, my friend, Mr Kerr's secretary. It was really through her that I heard about this job."

"I see." For some undefinable reason he appeared to relax visibly. "Well, to put the record straight, it was my father's business, not mine. Not until he disappeared six months ago on his yacht. I've been abroad most of the time. I'm an engineer."

"I'm sorry," Sara said slowly. It seemed strange that James hadn't mentioned it, but apparently he hadn't thought it necessary. If only she had known it would have saved her this temporary embarrassment.

Hugh Fraser's eyes narrowed. He said gently but with a firm note in his deep voice, "All this is irrelevant as far as you're concerned. If you like we can argue about the time later. I'm afraid the shock of my father's death was too much for my uncle who was older and not in good health. He loved Lochgoil, but I didn't realize how much he'd let things go until I came to sort out his affairs."

He paused and Sara looked away, carefully suppressing another murmur of sympathy, feeling instinctively that it wouldn't be welcome. He was talking to her now because of her job. "Old people invariably neglect their business," she pointed out, remembering some of her father's older patients.

He ignored this and went on wryly, "I'm afraid that when I saw the muddle in my uncle's study I immediately sent James Kerr a cry for help, but it was impossible to discuss details until you arrived. Apart from the clerical side there's something else I want to talk to you about before we reach Lochgoil."

"A good secretary is nothing if not versatile," Sara quoted weakly, while attempting to hide a sudden nervousness with a bright smile.

He stubbed his finished cigarette. "Mrs Scott, my housekeeper, will probably think so," he frowned absently. "And she'll no doubt consider it her duty to keep an eye on you. So be warned."

In spite of her tiredness Sara chuckled. She usually got on well with older people. "Is she elderly?" she asked, meeting his dark eyes with renewed confidence.

"In her sixties, I believe." His brow creased resignedly. "Biddy's a bit of an institution. Almost like one of the family, I suppose, and she likes her own way."

"Mr Kerr did mention your stepsister," Sara ventured cautiously. "He said you needed someone to help look after her."

She noticed that his face darkened fractionally as she spoke, and his expression was a mixture of resignation and impatience. "Jill is only twenty," he told her. "Her mother is in America on a long visit—she is actually American by birth, and Jill is supposed to be left in my care."

"Is there no one else?"

"More suitable, you mean?" His eyes glinted derisively as Sara flushed. "No one with any influence, I'm afraid."

Sara shot him a quick glance as his firm lips tightened. "You sound as if you have a problem."

"I could have," he agreed drily. "And it's one which I could well have done without. Jill appears to have got herself involved with rather a wild set since her mother left. Unfortunately," he sighed, "I've been too busy, and Jill just hasn't enough to do."

Sara couldn't help wondering why his sister hadn't gone to America with her mother. Surely such a trip would prove more exciting than a few off-beat friends? "It's probably just a phase," she suggested tactfully, turning her gaze from his frowning face to where his hands lay lightly on the steering wheel.

17

"Spare me the platitudes," his face was cynical. "You don't know my sister. She doesn't go through phases. She thinks she knows all the answers, yet manages to remain completely irresponsible. At the moment she imagines she's in love with a penniless artist, and is determined to marry him."

Sara's eyes swung back startled to his face. Obviously from the tone of his voice he disapproved. Was it the artist, she wondered, or his financial status? "If he's otherwise all right," she murmured uncertainly, "he might not always be penniless?"

"You could try listening to me, Miss Winton." He slewed around in his seat, catching her eyes, wide and unguarded, his own sardonic. "You've come a long way, and you're probably too tired to think straight. You could allow yourself to be guided by me. I do happen to have certain information. What I've heard of this young man leaves a lot to be desired. And that's putting it mildly."

"But have you met him?" she asked swiftly. The weight of his body was only inches from her own, but mentally she felt they were poles apart. Her pulse suddenly, inexplicably missed another beat. She felt sorry for the erring Jill.

He dealt with her query decisively, his eyes glinting as they narrowed over her. "I'm only concerned with Jill's impulsiveness. She is just getting over an operation and is coming to Lochgoil to convalesce. No one here knows anything about this particular boy-friend, so unless she does so herself, I don't think we need mention him. Probably if she doesn't see him for a while she'll forget all about him. But this is where I must have your help. I hardly think that he'll follow her here, but I need someone to keep an eye on her, and report to me if they see anything suspicious. I don't think that you'll find this a particularly arduous task."

Sara frowned, still not convinced. She had an uneasy feeling that she hadn't heard the whole story, that he was holding something back. It all sounded a bit too melodramatic, like some tale from the Middle Ages, and surely a more sympathetic approach would be better than this 'heavy father' act. Probably with Jill's mother away, his sense of responsibility had thrown him a little off balance. She said, "Couldn't you be somewhat prejudiced? Your sister and this man might be genuinely in love."

"I've already told you that it's impossible." His voice clipped short, his whole attitude inflexible. "Will you do as I ask?"

Hadn't he ever been in love himself? Sara wondered. She doubted it. A man like this would have his emotions under rigid control. His heart would only be allowed to soften according to the dictates of his head —and that would not be much.

When she didn't reply immediately he repeated his question impatiently, his voice hardening.

"I refuse to spy," Sara retorted, as sharply as she dared. Their eyes met, the air was taut with antagonism.

"I'm not asking you to spy. Don't be ridiculous!" Exasperated, he ran terse fingers through his thick dark hair, as if irritated by the whole situation. "If there was anything, of course, I should expect you to tell me, but not to exaggerate small incidents out of all proportion."

"Is that an order?"

"It could be."

"And if I don't agree?" Sara quailed inwardly, even while her eyes sparkled with indignation.

He said thinly, his gaze cold on her flushed face, "I wouldn't want to make an issue of it, but employees are usually prepared to obey orders."

"Within limits!" The words tumbled rebelliously from Sara's lips.

His answer came with chilling swiftness. "I ought to have seen you in London myself!"

Sara knew intuitively that no one had openly defied him before. She heard a voice—her own. "All right, you win. As I'm here I've not much option. I'll do what I can." Her capitulation was swift, but not noticeably graceful. She felt mutinous.

"Good." Now he was smiling, the smile of a man used to getting his way. He was prepared to be generous and disregard her unaccountable behaviour. "I think you'll find there won't be much to do, other than stopping Jill from running back to London every time she gets bored. Now we'll get on our way." He dismissed the subject as he flicked the starter, reversing sharply, shattering the silence. "I take it you won't mind working for me," he said smoothly, above the noise of the engine.

Sara's blue eyes smouldered as the Land-Rover swung around. She was stung by both his words and his manner, but decided to ignore his subtle reprisal. He must know that he wasn't being absolutely fair, but how could she argue the finer points of a situation which, on the face of it, seemed relatively simple? If Jill and her boy-friend really were in love it didn't seem likely that they wouldn't attempt to see each other, and if something like this should happen he couldn't possibly hold her responsible.

"When does your sister arrive?" she asked coolly as she clutched the edge of her seat to regain her balance.

He smiled a little ironically at her tangible air of hostility. "In a week or so, I expect. She's staying in London until she's well enough to travel, which should give us time to get started."

"Of course." It took an effort, but Sara concentrated on the view again. She felt slightly giddy as she dragged her eyes away from him. He was darkly, vividly masculine, with eyes like summer lightning, missing nothing. She added, defensively, "I'm used to long hours and hard work."

"You'd better be." His eyes licked over her sharply, noting the flare of colour beneath her smooth skin. "This won't exactly be a holiday. There appears to be about five years' work to catch up on. My uncle was obviously getting too old to cope."

"Aren't you being a little unkind?" She tilted her small head coolly. "Was there no one to help him?" She didn't dare ask where he had been himself. Probably in some far-off corner of the universe, judging by the mahogany colour of his skin.

He smiled, a little ironically, correctly construing her unspoken reproach, but making no attempt to explain his absence. Again he looked at her narrowly. "It seems to me, Sara, that you're too fond of asking questions! My uncle was no office man, as you will see. He preferred to spend his time out of doors."

She regretted the quick heat in her cheeks but couldn't control it. The sound of her own name almost shocked her. She stared down at her slim fingers. She needed a moment's respite to marshal her thoughts. There was a streak of hard ruthlessness in Hugh Fraser which she couldn't yet cope with. He would be used to working on huge projects abroad, and his staff would be hand-picked, highly geared and versatile. Any order he gave would be carried out with absolute efficiency. She doubted whether she could ever match up.

He regarded her still face obliquely with a negligent shrug of his powerful shoulders. "And what conclusions have you arrived at in that beautiful head of yours, dear Miss Winton?"

Anger leapt like a flame. He was a mocking devil, and he did it with such fine carelessness! Every nerve inside her tightened. She tried to speak evenly.

"I was hoping that we can work together amiably, Mr Fraser."

His eyes glinted with sudden amusement. "I'm sure we shall, Miss Winton. Providing you measure up to my requirements, I certainly won't complain."

"Have no fear, I will." Even if it kills me, her expression rounded off, as she stared at his dark profile with helpless intensity.

She couldn't remember being so aware of a man before. Everything about him, the imperious tilt of his head, the breadth of his shoulders, the deep cleft of his chin was vibrantly male. It was inevitable that he should antagonize women, yet in a curious fashion her eyes kept returning to him as they drove quickly along the lonely island road.

He pointed out various landmarks briefly as they passed them. There was the air-strip about a mile and a half from Salen. "It's useful," he said smoothly, "when I have to fly to London. Jill uses it quite a lot."

But he whipped her quickly through Salen itself, leaving her with only a hasty impression of houses and hotels huddled side by side in rather a beautiful village. She was aware of his sudden impatience to be on, ill-concealed by the pressure of his foot on the accelerator.

Once through Salen the road cut across the island

to the west coast, and in the late afternoon they reached Lochgoil. Sara always remembered her first glimpse of the castle, lying as it did on the edge of the sea, its massive stone bastions seeming a part of the landscape. Built of pink granite and creamy sandstone, it stood on the cliff-top, four-square to the winds, the westering sun turning to gold its turrets and towers.

He glanced at her startled face. "Does such a place scare you, Miss Winton? Perhaps I should have warned you what to expect?"

She looked away so that he could only see the pure curve of her cheek. "I don't scare easily," she murmured quietly.

"Don't you?" His voice held the slightest hint of menace, while his eyes appraised her coolly, clearly with mock exasperation. "Do you always find it necessary to double up like a hedgehog? You're about as prickly as one too."

"Self-defence, Mr Fraser. Although I resent the comparison." She turned to look at him, and as quickly looked away. His eyes were mocking, totally out of sympathy. Her heart had flooded with admiration at the sight of his castle. She might have confessed to love at first sight, but not now.

He picked up her sharp retort and tacked on casually, "Or a love affair that went wrong, Miss Winton? The symptoms are familiar enough to be recognizable, including the defence mechanism."

She said fiercely in undertone, "You couldn't be more completely wrong."

"I've yet to find myself completely wrong about anything," he replied with extreme dryness.

Stung, she flashed back at him, "That has nothing at all to do with it!"

"It could have," he taunted her. "And whoever it

was who left that intriguing hint of pathos in your face certainly made a good job of it."

Her heart jumped. She still couldn't talk about her parents without risking her somewhat precarious self-control, and she didn't want him to guess. Better that he should think what he was thinking than know the truth. She didn't want his commiseration. She only wanted to forget.

"I suggest we call a truce, Miss Winton." He glanced at her with the hint of a smile. "You have a sharp tongue when provoked."

He negotiated a huge stone archway with the practiced twist of familiarity, driving into a wide paved courtyard. He was obviously unperturbed, but she still felt as taut as stretched wire.

Thankfully she realized they had arrived. Now, perhaps, she could escape him while she marshalled her thoughts. He had said, a short time ago, that he regretted not having interviewed her himself, but never again, she vowed, would she take a job without first meeting her future employer. Although she doubted if many would be as unconventional as Hugh Fraser!

A funny little nerve jumped in the base of her throat, and his eyes rested on it briefly as they drew up. "If you're quite ready," he said, as she hesitated nervously, "perhaps you would like to come and meet Biddy. You'll probably approve of her more than you do me."

"Of course," she smiled at him, portraying a coolness she didn't feel, trying to match his satire but failing hopelessly.

His right eyebrow rose slightly and she flushed hotly, making his triumph complete as they walked silently across the flagstones into the house.

CHAPTER TWO

DETERMINED that he shouldn't upset her any further, Sara followed Hugh Fraser briskly into the castle. She walked behind him down a long barrel-vaulted ground-floor corridor, through a door which opened straight into a great square hall with a stone-flagged floor. On the floor of the hall lay some rugs, while against the walls pieces of tapestry hung above high carved chests. On one of these chests stood a huge jug of tall yellow tulips, their bright colour glowing through the dim light from the narrow windows. At one end a wheel stair contained within the thickness of the wall rose to the floor above. This was covered by a thick red carpet.

"Welcome to Lochgoil," Hugh Fraser murmured smoothly behind her.

She turned to look at him, not speaking, and he noticed her startled expression. "You'll soon get used to it," he added, smiling. "It seems big, but once you can find your way around you soon forget about the size. We're really very comfortable, you'll find."

"Of course," she replied quickly, finding her voice as he took her arm and drew her firmly over the flagstones, up the stone staircase to the hall on the first floor.

Sara felt immediately better. Here three high windows set in deep round-arched embrasures gave more than adequate light and rapidly dispersed the gloomy impression of the entrance chamber. In a spacious fireplace, wide and deep, with decorated aumbries in its jambs, a fragrant log fire burnt cheerfully. Around this hall carved oaken doors obviously led to living rooms, while again, at the farthermost end, another staircase twisted upwards.

"We live mostly on this floor and the next." He released her tense arm with an amused lift of dark eyebrows, but before she could reply one of the doors across the hall opened and a small neat-looking woman emerged from what was evidently the kitchen. "Ah, here comes Biddy," he said, with what to Sara's sensitive ears seemed almost like a sigh of relief.

She turned as Biddy walked towards her. Biddy was certainly small, but she possessed a rather grim dignity which seemed to give her height. She had the unmistakable air of a woman used to giving orders and being obeyed, yet her face held a definite kindness. Sara liked her at once.

She held out her hand and Biddy took it as Hugh introduced them.

"I hope you will find the castle to your liking, miss," she said politely, her keen eyes on Sara's flushed cheeks. "I'll ring for Katie to take you to your room. I expect you're tired after your journey." Her hand went out to a bell in the wall without waiting for Sara to reply.

"I'm not in any hurry," Sara demurred quietly, feeling a somewhat alien desire to assert herself. Irrationally she felt she was being pushed around, first by Hugh Fraser, and now Biddy.

Deliberately, she thought, he chose to misunderstand as his glinting eyes met hers. "You can talk to Biddy later, and she'll show you around. In the meantime I think you would be wise to do as she suggests. You've certainly had a long day."

"Mr Hugh's right." Biddy nodded her silver-grey

head, smiling approvingly. "And you'll feel much better tomorrow after a good night's rest. Then you'll find there's plenty to do."

"I'll certainly try to be useful." Sara looked quickly away from him, addressing Biddy. "If there's anything I can do to help . . .?"

Her voice trailed off uncertainly and she didn't have to look at Hugh Fraser to see his derisive expression. An uneasy surge of rebellion shook her as she smoothed a hand rather wearily across her forehead. Biddy clearly hung on his every word, but he couldn't expect her to do the same.

Biddy, not aware of undercurrents, nodded again and said soothingly, "Katie won't be a minute, Miss Winton. Sometimes, I'm afraid, she seems to get lost."

Feeling it futile to say more, Sara smiled and waited silently for the absent Katie. She gazed around with renewed interest as Biddy turned to discuss with Hugh Fraser a man who had called earlier while he was out.

She had never lived in a place as old as this before, and she wondered, faintly apprehensive, how she would like it. The castle must be literally hundreds of years old, seventeenth century, most probably, and there must surely be a ghost or two lurking around those shadowy passages. But someone at some time had carefully modernized the interior of the building, cleverly combining the old with the new. In this spacious hall everything was in the best of taste with solid comfort everywhere. All designed for perfect living, she thought wryly, as Katie came and whisked her up the next flight of stairs to her room.

Her bedroom, she found, was in one of the round towers. Not in any sense modern, but unusual and charming. Her feet sank into a warm, rose-coloured carpet, and there was a rose-patterned chintz bedspread and armchair to match. On a small table beside the chair lay a pile of books and magazines, and an electric radiator spread a welcome warmth. Somehow, in spite of the difference, it reminded Sara of her mother's guest room at home.

Katie glanced down at the table. Like Biddy she had looked Sara carefully over and seemed to approve. "You might like to sit here sometimes," she grinned at Sara cheerfully, "so I left some magazines."

Sara, hastily swallowing a twinge of nostalgia, thanked her gratefully. Although no one had actually said so Katie was obviously the maid. Sara liked her round merry face, the bright intelligent eyes and gay friendly smile. She disappeared, but returned almost immediately with a tea-tray laden with a steaming pot of tea and hot buttered toast.

"Biddy sent this," she said breathlessly. "And I'm to tell you that dinner is at seven."

Later, after she had bathed and rested a little, Sara put on a soft afternoon dress and went downstairs again.

Dinner, she found, was served in a small dining room just off the hall, but she ate in solitary splendour. Hugh Fraser was nowhere to be seen. As she sat alone at the long polished table she wished, rather belatedly, that she had asked for a tray in her room.

Afterwards Biddy came to see if Katie had brought her everything she needed and lingered while Sara drank her coffee in the hall.

"Mr Hugh's dining with friends," she told Sara, who had wondered but not liked to ask Katie. "He often goes out. There's not much company for him here at the moment, but of course it will be different when Miss Jill arrives. I hope you don't mind, miss?"

Sara didn't. On her own she had felt a sense of

relief which was hard to explain. In any case she could scarcely object as to how her employer spent his time. But perhaps Biddy wouldn't realize this. She had probably never had to deal with a secretary before.

Tactfully she tried to change the subject. "I expect I'll soon get used to living here," she said, smiling. "I suppose you've lived here a long time yourself?"

"Now that the estate belongs to Mr Hugh some of us might not be here much longer," Biddy retorted sharply. The words seemed to escape her lips accidentally, almost as if they had been bottled up too long. "Of course," she went on hastily, looking intently at Sara, "we do understand that he might have to sell Lochgoil, or even employ younger workers. Some of the employees are getting old, I'm afraid, and one or two, like myself, are plagued with rheumatism." Unconsciously emphasizing her point, she rubbed her hands over her narrow hips with a sigh.

Sara put down her coffee cup and stared at her, startled. She had hoped to steer the conversation away from Hugh Fraser, but it bounced back at her like a rubber ball. Surely he wouldn't think of depriving these elderly people of their homes, even if his uncle had foolishly made no provision for them? Frowning, she considered Biddy's fragile bones, feeling strangely at loss for words.

"Mr Fraser must spend a lot of his time abroad," she said at last, making a rather groping effort of reassurance. "Wouldn't it be better if you were here to look after the house while he was away?"

"Maybe he'll get married and his wife will do that!" Biddy refused to be comforted. "He's very popular with the ladies, you know. And there's one in particular who is in France at the moment. She likes him very much indeed."

Sara digested this in silence, unable to account for the little tremor that ran through her nerves. "Perhaps Miss Jill will be able to help?" Diplomatically she tried to ignore Biddy's cryptic remarks, putting them down to the woman's over-anxious state of mind. Hugh Fraser's matrimonial plans couldn't possibly concern his secretary, as Biddy must know very well. She was in no position to offer an opinion, even if she had one, but surely there must be someone to whom Biddy could turn for advice? It seemed strange and not a little puzzling that Biddy should have to confide in a comparative stranger.

But it appeared that Biddy was already regretting her impulsive remarks. She turned quickly away, picking up Sara's empty coffee cup as she went. "I would not like to bother Miss Jill," she muttered. "I've no doubt that Mr Hugh will settle all our difficulties, given time."

With that she disappeared through the green baize door into the kitchen, calling over her shoulder that Sara was to ring for Katie if she required anything further. She had apparently forgotten that she was to show Sara around the castle. That, Sara concluded as she gazed at the gently swinging door, must obviously wait until another day.

Sara was surprised to find she slept dreamlessly that night, and when she awoke it took her some time to gather her senses and realize where she was. The knowledge came to her with a sense of shock. Lochgoil Castle. Those thick, grim stone walls! But her bed was comfortable and sunshine poured in through the half-open window. Thrusting back the sheets, she ran over to look out. The view was magnificent from her round tower; on this side the sea was a vast shimmering expanse of blue. Looking down, close to the shore, she could see small bays and inlets with white sandy beaches. It all looked very inviting.

Quickly she splashed her face with cold water and hurried into her clothes, choosing her old jeans again and a matching slim-fit shirt. Hugh Fraser had sent a message via Katie late the evening before that he would see her in the library after breakfast. It was still very early, barely seven o'clock. Sara glanced at her watch. She had plenty of time to explore.

On the outside corridor she slid her feet into a pair of light sandals and ran down the twisting stairways. There wasn't a soul about. The huge castle was silent; Sara thought she could have heard a pin drop. Ignoring the imposing front entrance, she went to the back of the hall, finding without much difficulty the long stone passage which she had traversed with Hugh Fraser not so many hours ago, and let herself noiselessly out into the courtyard.

Here again nothing stirred. She felt she had the whole world to herself as she stepped out into a perfect spring morning. Finding her way around the corner of the castle, she walked to the cliff edge and stared down on to the rocks below. The tide was well out and between ribs of black rock lay deep green pools, but less sand than she had thought from her bedroom window. This must be Loch na Keal, she decided, gazing across the sun-flecked waters to where the slopes of Ben More fell gently into flat strips of ground by the farther shore. At this side she hadn't realized that the cliffs would be so high, but there must be a way down to that enticing shore.

Ensnared by so much beauty, she turned and walked until she came to a narrow cleft in the rock, where what appeared to be a track, now almost overgrown, descended on to the beach. It had obviously not been used for years.

Without stopping to think Sara pushed determinedly through the undergrowth, thrusting aside the dead briars, trying to get a foothold on ground made slippery by recent rain. All at once, perhaps because she sensed that time was getting on, it seemed imperative that she should reach the beach. A thorn caught painfully at her hair, snatching the ribbon she had used to tie it back, so that it clouded her face and she could scarcely see where she was going. She slid the last few yards, but to her dismay when she picked herself up she still had some way to go. She was caught on a narrow ledge! Above her the path hung almost vertical, while below was a drop of several feet down a smooth cliff face.

Bewildered, Sara pushed back her unruly hair with a hand that wasn't quite steady. This wasn't turning out exactly as she had planned. Glancing upwards over her shoulder, she saw that it would be impossible to get back the way she had come, and equally impossible to lower herself down on to the rocks below without probably breaking a leg. In her imagination she saw herself being packed off home in an ambulance and gulped convulsively with a shudder of dismay. Her behaviour this morning would be put down as inexcusable if Hugh Fraser had anything to do with it!

Panic swept inevitably through her. The ledge was both narrow and uncomfortable and provided little shelter against a cool rising wind off the sea. A coldness penetrated her thin shirt, finding her bare skin, and she huddled against the rock in an effort to keep warm. Nearer the water-line she could see some small duck-like birds and a few black guillemots diving amongst them, but there was no sign of any human inhabitant. She tried shouting, but no one came. If there was anyone around they would never hear, Sara thought dismally, above the pounding of the waves.

Taking three deep breaths, her parents' own personal remedy for panic, she tried to change her cramped position. Someone was sure to come, she told herself firmly, it was ridiculous to feel so frightened, but all she could see was Hugh Fraser's sardonic face. What on earth would he say if he ever heard about this? She could imagine his scathing remarks!

To her utter consternation she hadn't long to wait. She heard the thunder of hooves on the sand seconds before she saw him coming and jumped wildly to her feet, almost losing her balance as she shouted to attract his attention.

Hugh Fraser curbed the big bay horse he rode sharply as he turned his dark head and saw her waving high above him. For one long withering moment he stared at her narrowly before pulling curtly at the reins and trotting over to stop just below her. "What the devil are you doing up there?" he shouted tersely. "I thought I'd hired a secretary, not a circus act!" His eyes plainly registered his disgust.

Sara's own eyes blazed as she looked down at him, and she clenched her fists, feeling the tell-tale colour creeping under her skin. She'd never felt so stupid in all her life, but couldn't he understand her predicament? Need he be so sarcastic? "I'm sorry," she shouted back indignantly, "I only tried to use the path."

"Didn't you see a notice or realize how high these cliffs are?" His eyes held hers, glinting impatiently. "That path hasn't been used for years, even a blind man could see that!"

"I didn't know . . ." With a visible effort Sara bit back a hastier retort, reforming her words into an almost reluctant plea for help. Why hadn't someone else come along? She would have welcomed anyone but Hugh Fraser. As her polite request for assistance floated sullenly between them she stared stormily down into his upturned face.

"If you twist around and lower yourself carefully over the edge I can reach you."

The arid tone of his voice was not lost on Sara, but she knew better than to argue. To get such an ordeal over as quickly as possible might reduce it to minimal proportions; besides, she was in no position to do other than follow his instructions. Drawing another deep breath, she did as she was told. For one awful moment as her feet swung into space she closed her eyes and her heart nearly stopped beating. Then just as her hands began to slip from their hold on the rock he caught her in a steel-like grip and swung her on to the front of his horse.

Sara shuddered uncontrollably and pushed back against the lean, powerful frame of the man who held her. His arm around her hurt with the strength of his grip as the big horse reared with the impact of her body and her eyes flew open. "Please put me down, Mr Fraser," she cried, her breath coming strangled in her throat as unconsciously, with agitated fingers, she tried to unravel the tangled strands of her hair.

But it was several minutes before he reined in slowly, then instead of releasing her he tightened his hold as he pointed to where the cliffs and the beach reached a more accessible level. "If you'd gone a little farther," he said drily, "you could have walked down to the sea quite easily and needn't have finished up as you did."

She turned her head from him, her profile delicate with tremulous pleading. "How was I to know?—I only arrived yesterday."

The observation sounded trite, even to her own ears, and she wasn't surprised when he retorted sharply, "All the more reason why you should have asked someone!"

There was logic in what he said, but in her present position she couldn't think straight. He was too close. She could feel the heavy beat of his heart against her shoulder, and the hardness of his body through the thin material of her shirt. She tried to draw away from him a little, but he seemed in no great hurry to put her down.

He continued his lecture, refusing to let her escape so easily. "You must try to remember that parts of this coast can be very dangerous. The cliffs are extremely high in places, and often loose. When I first came here as a boy the path you found did go down to the shore, but since then a lot of the cliff face has fallen away and people who stupidly try to use it usually get caught."

"So I'm not the first?"

"Nor the last, I suppose. People never cease to amaze me." His dark brows drew together. "The coastline of Mull shouldn't be likened to that of an English seaside resort."

Sara bristled. Did he intend to be insulting? He certainly believed in speaking his mind! Of course he did have every right to be furious. She had been extremely foolish and was wasting his valuable time. But he hadn't even bothered to ask if she was any the worse, so he couldn't accuse her of wasting his sympathy! A sharp twinge of self-pity smote her as she stared down at the horse's reddish-brown mane, her blue eyes mutinous.

As if he was perfectly aware of her resentment Hugh Fraser's gaze fixed itself on her face with a hint of irony. "I trust you aren't suffering from exposure?" She stiffened as his eyes went deliberately over her, noting her dishevelled appearance. Then, apparently satisfied that she was relatively unscathed, he went on before she could protest. "Do you realize that you're due to start work in less than an hour?"

"I can't if you won't put me down," she choked defensively. But again he took no notice as he urged the big horse up the steep gradient from the beach. As she jerked back against him she could feel his breath warm on her cheek, and his fingers taut where they held her slim waist fast in front of him.

Once on top of the cliffs she saw that the castle was farther away than she had thought. She felt the leashed impatience in him as he pointed towards it brusquely. "You can see your way now, and when you do come down again watch the tides. You could be cut off quite suddenly and I might not be on hand to rescue you another time." His fingers caught her bare nape as he brushed back her hair which the wind blew in his face, and the contact sent a million prickles racing down her spine.

"I'm sure that won't be necessary," Sara retorted, her cheeks scarlet at his controlled cynicism. "Perhaps it would be better if I didn't leave the castle grounds." A certain prudence warned her that she was being particularly ungracious to her boss, but for the first time in her life she found herself speaking without any discretion.

He chose to ignore her outburst. There was only the painful jerk of his arm as he pulled to a halt, which might or might not have been intentional. "What sort of people did you work for previously?" he asked smoothly, as he lowered her to the ground. "I'm beginning to wonder."

"My parents," Sara returned starkly, as she regained her balance and straightened carefully. It still hurt to mention them, and if James hadn't explained about the plane crash—and there was no reason to suppose that he had—then she didn't intend saying anything herself.

Her eyes darkened as he observed drily, "Were they wise to turn you loose, I wonder?"

Sara stared up at him, meeting his mocking gaze. His relaxed seat in the saddle belied his absolute control over the huge bay horse. Did he expect to control women the same way? She refused to answer his last question. Sympathy must not be allowed to pave the way for her, even if this morning's escapade hadn't already doomed her chances. Besides, ever since she had stepped off the boat he seemed to have been hinting subtly of her unsuitability. Did he already want to be rid of her?

She looked away from him with a scarcely audible sigh, her voice full of unconscious pleading. "I can only ask you to give me another chance. You can't possibly send me home because of this one incident."

"Not an auspicious beginning, you must admit." His hard mouth twisted wryly. "However, we'll see how things go. The chances of finding someone else at this late hour are remote, and I'm relying on you to look after my sister." His glance still lingered on her pale face and sharpened intently. "Right now I suggest you go and get something to eat, or you'll not be fit for anything this morning."

His broad shoulders lifted dismissively beneath his

thick sweater, and Sara fled without another word, not stopping until she reached her room.

Breathlessly ignoring a longing to throw herself on her bed, she threw off her rock-stained clothes and rinsed her hot face. Her side still hurt from the cruel grip of Hugh Fraser's hands as he had hauled her on to his horse. A highway brigand might have been kinder! She winced a little both from pain and humiliation as she drew a neat navy dress over her head and combed her tangled hair into gleaming order. Her reflection in the mirror was trim and businesslike, and she hoped rather bitterly that he would approve.

In the dining room where breakfast was laid she only took time for a cup of coffee and one piece of toast before asking Katie where she might find the library.

"Straight along the hall, miss. It's the last door on the right." She was obviously put out when Sara refused to eat any more. "Miss Jill always eats a good breakfast when she comes. She says the air gives her an appetite." She eyed Sara's empty plate disapprovingly.

Sara smiled but didn't stop to argue or try to explain about her foolish adventure on the cliffs. That was something which she only wanted to forget, and Katie, like Hugh Fraser, might not be at all sympathetic.

She hurried down the hall and knocked carefully on the library door. As she had feared, he was already there and she was conscious of his swift glance of appraisal as she walked into the room. Had he expected her old blue jeans? She was glad that her hair was tidy and that she had applied a minimum of make-up.

He dispensed with preliminaries, getting straight

38

down to work, making no reference to their earlier meeting on the beach. He indicated a small desk by the window. "I've had it specially brought in for you," he told her. "There's not much room to spare on this." Frowning, he contemplated the littered top of the larger desk at which he sat.

Sara followed the direction of his gaze with bewilderment. Piles of correspondence were stacked everywhere and the large, capacious drawers seemed full to overflowing. Well, he had warned her!

While he waited passively she crossed the room, sitting down self-consciously, tucking her long legs neatly beneath her chair, hoping fervently that she would be able to cope. She had never seen such a muddle before. In the surgery at home everything had been systematically filed. She wondered what her parents would have thought of this!

"I collected that from London a few days ago." He watched while she removed the cover from a new portable typewriter. "My uncle apparently had no use for such things, but I don't think we could manage without one."

As Sara smiled politely and studied the machine with interest, he picked up some hastily scribbled notes. "To begin with I'd like to dictate a few rather urgent letters which you can type while I'm out after lunch."

Sara picked up her pad in readiness, only to find that he had laid his notes down again as he paused reflectively, his eyes on her face. "It might be easier if you understood, Miss Winton," he said with emphasis, "that as well as the backlog here I have a sizeable farm to run, so I don't have unlimited time to devote to this lot. I shall probably have to leave you quite often to manage on your own, as I expect

James Kerr told you."

"He did say you were busy."

"That's putting it mildly!" He reached impatiently for a cigarette and matches, tipping back his chair as he inhaled deeply, staring at her narrowly through the smoke. "There are times when you might feel overworked, but when I go down to London you can forget most of this and play with Jill. Explore the island together. Jill knows it very well and will enjoy showing you around."

Her chin tilted sharply with annoyance. He talked as if she was ten years old. Was he trying to run her life as well as Jill's? "I expect we'll think of something," she retorted coolly.

"In the meantime your hours here will be erratic." His eyes briefly touched her mutinous mouth. "Sometimes I work in the evenings, after dinner. I hope you won't mind?"

Sara disliked his habit of issuing an order in the guise of a question to which she couldn't possibly object. In all fairness, Sara conceded, he must be very busy with all his different enterprises, and now that he had mentioned them himself this might be a good chance to put a word in about Biddy and Katie. Even so, how could she ask about their future on her first day here? He might well think it sheer impertinence if nothing worse. But in spite of her doubts she couldn't help asking impulsively, "Do you intend to farm Lochgoil yourself?"

"I might, eventually." His eyes glinted slightly, as if he guessed a little of what she was thinking, "But I didn't anticipate having to change jobs at my time of life. I'm quite a good engineer."

He would be! Sara's nerves tensed. He would be satisfied with nothing less than top-rate efficiency in both himself and others.

The telephone rang, shattering the momentary silence, and she was aware of his steady regard as he picked up the receiver.

As he talked her eyes strayed from his impatient face around the book-lined room to where a huge, single log smouldered sulkily in a massive stone fireplace. A beautifully patterned but faded carpet covered most of the old oak floorboards, and two big leather armchairs stood on either side of the wide hearth. Sara could imagine the snug comfort of the room in winter with the heavy curtains drawn against the wild Atlantic gales.

Lochgoil must be an attractive proposition for any man. How would Hugh Fraser decide? Sara's eyes returned to his dark face, surprised by her own eagerness, not entirely because of his employees on the estate. Her own curiosity was too near the surface and, she told herself severely, ought not to be functioning in his direction at all, especially on such short acquaintance!

"That was the chap I dined with last night." Sara almost jumped as he replaced the receiver abruptly and returned to his notes. His thick brows drew together sharply as he glanced up. "He particularly wants to see me after lunch. A small business matter has cropped up, so perhaps we'd better forget about anything else and get on."

During the next few days Sara felt she might well have been glued to her office chair, with her whole life revolving around her typewriter. If Hugh Fraser was satisfied with her efforts he failed to say so, but Sara consoled herself with the thought that at least he didn't complain. In the mornings he dictated and left numerous instructions. After lunch she sorted and filed. By tea time she usually had most of the work cleared and the letters typed ready for his signature. Sometimes she saw a light burning late beneath the library door as she went up to bed, but so far he had not asked her to join him. The evenings she mostly spent reading and doing odd jobs for Biddy, who sometimes suffered painfully from her rheumatism. Biddy had a fund of stories about her childhood on the island, and Sara felt more than repaid for her labours as she listened to her.

"You ought to get out more," Biddy said sharply, coming to the end of a particularly long tale and noting Sara's pale cheeks with some concern. "The evenings are nice now, you ought to take a walk occasionally, not sit with an old woman, Miss Sara."

But Sara had not gone down to the sea again, not after that first morning, although why, she could not say. Instead she contented herself with exploring the castle, studying the early architecture with inexpert but growing interest, and getting to know some of the other people who worked out on the farm.

"I do go out sometimes," she protested, glancing at Biddy, smiling. "But there's plenty to keep me busy here."

"I do know that!" Biddy's frown deepened instead of disappearing as Sara had hoped it would, as she went on. "Mr Hugh certainly believes in hard work, but his uncle would hardly look at a bit o' correspondence if he could help it, and he's left quite a muddle behind him, and no mistake. His accountant, poor man, had an awful time with him, but Mr Fraser would only laugh and promise to do better, but he never did. Mr Hugh, now, he's a different kettle of fish altogether. No doubt he'll soon get things sorted out . . ." She paused, still frowning at Sara dubiously,

"It's the future that I keep worrying about, as I told you. You see, at my age one takes badly to changes."

As Sara rose to go upstairs she couldn't help wondering why Biddy should persist in confiding in her. She could only imagine that Biddy was nervous about approaching Hugh herself, and vaguely hoped that a word from Sara, as his secretary, might solve her difficulties. Surely it must be quite clear that she had no more influence than anyone else on the estate, probably not as much. Sara doubted if Hugh ever really noticed her outside office hours.

One morning several days later he asked her to go with him to Tobermory. She was gazing wistfully through the office window, unaware that he was watching her until he said crisply, "I'm going to Tobermory this afternoon and I'd like you to come with me. That's really an order."

Sara didn't intend to argue, the bright May sunshine was too tempting. An unexpected glow of pleasure surged through her veins even while her eyes strayed guiltily to the piles of correspondence still to be sorted.

His eyes followed the direction of hers impatiently. "You've managed to get through quite a lot of work since you started, Miss Winton, but I don't expect you to remain here without a break."

Sara felt herself colouring faintly. It was the sort of back-handed compliment at which he excelled! Did he suppose that she might jump to the wrong conclusions if he showed more than a lukewarm appreciation? Well, he needn't worry. She only wanted to finish this job as quickly as possible and get back to London. His remarks when he had rescued her from the cliffs had proved quite clearly that he had little time for a girl like herself. But for a few hours it might be fun to take advantage of his impersonal offer and see something of the island before she left it for ever!

As she slowly murmured her consent he crossed to the door, smiling a shade sharply. "I'll see you after lunch, then," he said.

CHAPTER THREE

SARA dressed quickly. She wore a shapely, short wool skirt with a matching blue sweater which clung neatly to the slender curves of her young figure. Brushing out her long fair hair she tied it loosely back, loving the freedom of it after the rather severe style which she had worn lately for work. A dusting of powder on her fine smooth skin, a dash of pink lipstick on her wide curved mouth and she was ready. Swiftly she ran downstairs.

Hugh wasn't there, so she waited in the hall, studying a Raeburn which hung beside the fireplace. She was no art expert, but Jane had taken her to one or two lectures in the Tate Gallery, and she recalled someone saying that they thought Raeburn's style a bit like Reynolds, who had been born earlier, but in the same century. It was surprising, she thought, gazing around, that so many valuable paintings should be hanging unprotected in the castle.

"A good dog is probably as good a deterrent as any," Hugh Fraser smiled, when she asked him about burglars as they started out. "But we don't seem to have many thieves in this part of the world. We might envy other people their possessions, but we rarely steal them."

"Your principles don't seem to apply to women," Sara retorted lightly. "Wasn't it here that young Lochinvar stole his lady-love?"

Hugh glanced at her laconically as he adjusted his seat-belt. "Aren't you thinking of Lord Ullin's daughter and her Highland chieftain? I think that Lochinvar operated somewhere else. In the Border country, I believe."

Hurriedly Sara concentrated on her own seat-belt, trying to ignore his raised eyebrows. "You could be right," she replied coolly. "It's a long time ago. Things like that don't happen any more."

His dark eyes still mocked as they drove smoothly away from the castle. "You might recall that you were carried off yourself by a wild Highlander the other morning."

Sara flushed as her pulse gave a traitorous jerk. "You're twisting the circumstances," she said shortly. "That was something quite different."

"I wonder?" His eyes flicked enigmatically from her face to the road. Along Loch na Keal the road turned right. Across the water opposite them lay Ulva. The surface of the sea between was flecked lightly by white horses. "Not far from here," Hugh waved his hand seaward, "on the Mull shore, is a grave alleged to be that of Lord Ullin's daughter and the Chief of Ulva. According to local legend they were wrecked while running away together as they crossed Loch na Keal from Gribun on the ferry. The poet, Thomas Campbell, probably heard the story when he worked here as a tutor in 1795."

"I remember the poem." Sara's blue eyes clouded as she stared out through the car window over the wild rocky headlands. She shivered. "Nothing seems to have changed, it might have happened yesterday."

"An island like this can be curiously timeless." Again Hugh flicked his hand. "If you look beyond Ulva you'll see more islands. There's Little Colonsay, Inch Kenneth, and the Treshnish group."

Entranced, Sara let her gaze wing towards them.

Pale lilac, low-set in a waste of seas, they lay west-wards across the horizon, on the edge of the world. The sheer beauty of the scene held her silent. It was places such as this that men wrote poems about, and wasn't it somewhere near here, on Staffa, that Mendelssohn wrote the overture Fingal's Cave?

She heard Hugh saying, "My uncle loved the Islands. The Hebrides! He was a Scot with a passionate love for his native land. It's a pity he didn't apply himself quite so assiduously to his own affairs."

The dryness of his tone didn't escape Sara, and for a moment she disliked him intensely. He might profess an interest in the past and be receptive to its romantic legends, but he would never allow himself to be influenced by it to any great extent. There was only so much of the dreamer about him. "Haven't you ever been at the mercy of your emotions?" she asked recklessly, a vivid likeness of the unfortunate Chief of Ulva springing clearly to her mind.

His eyes touched her lightly. "Come now, Sara, you couldn't expect me to answer that one!"

His use of her name blotted out the evasiveness of his reply. A warm confusion swept over her. 'Sara' was a welcome change from 'Miss Winton', but it seemed to put their relationship on an entirely different footing. Her eyes widened uncertainly. Her comparatively sheltered existence hadn't armed her with a mental resilience adept enough to cope with a man of his calibre. For the first time in her life she felt emotionally disturbed by a man, and at loss for words.

The sun struck obliquely across the side of his head. He gave the impression of great vigour and what she construed to herself as ruthlessness. He threw her another glance, a wicked gleam in his eyes, as if he was entirely aware of her inexperience and amused by it. "From now on I'm going to call you Sara. Miss Winton is too time-consuming."

Sara looked carefully away from that tantalizing smile. "Of course," she murmured. "I hope your sister will, too." The road swung darkly. She sensed that her conventional little speech would divert him and felt her nerves tighten with resentment. She turned to him, her eyes smouldering. "You enjoy teasing me," she said faintly, controlling her anger with difficulty, trying to remember her position.

He smiled, a real smile this time with laughter springing to his eyes, not just a twist of his ironic mouth. "You're too provoking," he replied lazily. "There's a lot to be said for the gentle art of retaliation, but sometimes you do answer back."

"You do happen to be my employer," she reminded him coldly.

"Tut, tut." He grinned again at her obvious displeasure. "Don't let such a small matter as that inhibit your natural impulses."

Sara could cheerfully have hit him! Could nothing penetrate the façade of his easy urbane manner? He played with words, treating them lightly, uncaringly, almost as if at times he enjoyed the discomfort they could inflict. "Have you heard from your sister yet?" Hastily suppressing her baser instincts, she clung tenaciously to safer grounds.

"Yes—that reminds me!" His humour appeared to desert him with startling suddenness. "Now that you've mentioned it, Jill rang after lunch. She arrives tomorrow."

"I'm looking forward to meeting her." In spite of her previous reluctance there was more than a hint of sincerity in Sara's voice. Jill might act as a buffer between herself and this man whose moods could swing like a pendulum between hard complacency and a disturbing tolerance.

He shrugged and she stared away from him out of the open window, attempting to steer her thoughts to safer channels. They were making their way up the west coast of the island towards the village of Burg and Calgary Bay. This way, Hugh told her, they would see something of the coastline before going on to Tobermory. The seaward views changed from headland to headland, the land seemed wilder, the moors bare and open.

Sara's eyes bright with interest travelled across the heather, then, without thinking, she clutched his arm so that the car swerved over the road as he applied the brakes. "I'm sorry," she gasped breathlessly, pointing to where a huge bird sat silently on top of a long pole. "I've never seen an eagle so near at hand before!"

"And you'll probably never see another if you make a habit of grabbing my arm like that when I'm driving!" His eyes followed hers to the telephone pole as he corrected the car and pulled into the side of the road. "I'm afraid you're going to feel disappointed. That's a buzzard, not an eagle. A lot of people make the same mistake."

Sara was too absorbed to manage more than a brief apology. "I'm sorry—about your arm, I mean. And the—buzzard. Are you quite sure?" She swung back to stare at him, a faintly perplexed look in her eyes.

He flexed his broad shoulders lightly, noting her doubtful expression. "The eagle," he explained, "is larger, with a wing span up to seven feet. It's dark brown too, but with a lot of golden brown on its crown and nape, whereas a buzzard, as you can see, is usually white underneath. There are more buzzards in the West Highlands and Wales than in any other region."

To her surprise he leant over in front of her and wound down the window. For a few seconds she was intensely aware of his body touching her own. "Won't it fly away?" she asked in a low voice, her breath catching unevenly in her throat, though whether because of the buzzard or Hugh Fraser's unexpected proximity she scarcely knew.

His eyebrows rose fractionally. As if unaware of her quickening pulses he kept his arm along the back of her seat, his fingers touching her shoulder. "I've seen them sit without moving for more than an hour, but if they do see something they fancy they can drop from their perch with great speed. They like rabbits and voles and such-like. I'm afraid the gamekeepers aren't very fond of them as they're said to take game, and a lot of them get shot."

"Aren't they protected?" Sara twisted around to meet his eyes indignantly.

"They are." His hand shifted as he moved slightly, "but sometimes the law isn't always effective, and can be difficult to enforce in a place such as this."

"Not exactly a paradise for birds." A cool wind from the sea caught her words and blew them softly through the wiry green grass. "Oh, look!" She jerked back against him, excitement replacing regret as the buzzard, apparently not appreciating the attention it was receiving, soared effortlessly into the air. The variegated pattern under its spread wings, caught by a flickering ray of sunlight, was a thing of beauty. Sara held her breath.

A slight smile touched his well cut mouth as his

gaze stayed momentarily on her animated face, so near his own, before turning to watch the huge bird settle on a rocky crag high above them. "They have a wing span of at least four feet, and the female is larger than the male." With a touch of finality he wound up the window and started the engine again. "If you're really interested we could go out one day and do a spot of bird-watching properly."

"When there's more time." She shaded her eyes against the bright sunlight. The buzzard disappeared from view as the road twisted up the side of the loch. He was too busy ever to have time!

"Time . . ." He frowned suddenly, as if he followed the silent trend of her thoughts. "I never seem to have enough of that, Sara."

"I suppose it rather depends what one wants from life. Cars like this, for instance." Her fingers curved uncertainly over the luxurious leather seat.

"You could be right." His eyes touched her fingers. "But this new Jaguar belonged to my uncle. It seemed easier than bringing my own."

Sara grimaced inwardly as he turned her ambiguous remark neatly back on her, although she was willing to bet that his own car would be no rattletrap. She felt sure he would demand the best, whether it was cars or women, and the thought was curiously disquieting.

"Do you drive, Sara?"

"Yes, I do." At home she still had the Mini which her parents had given her on her last birthday.

"If you can manage this, you can borrow it sometimes. In fact I'll let you drive after tea. You'll soon get the hang of it."

Her eyes were suddenly brilliant, because she was young and rather reckless beneath the protective veneer of passivity engendered by the events of the past few weeks. "Aren't you afraid I'll do something silly?" She smiled happily, her smile a dazzling whiteness across her animated face.

"I was beginning to think you never would." He considered her for a moment with evident amusement, noting at a glance the sparkling change of her expression. "Perhaps we shall see the chrysalis emerging yet!"

Sara sobered instantly. Why must he put a damper on everything? But perhaps it was her own fault, allowing herself to be so ridiculously pleased by the idea of driving this car. Yet his remark did strike a responsive chord deep within her, a zest for living which she had not known for weeks. And it might be better to remember that he probably enjoyed teasing her as he would his young sister, baiting her with subtle raillery against which her best defence would be indifference.

Stubbornly, as she sensed he awaited a sharp retort, she remained smiling but silent, but felt inordinately relieved to see that they were approaching Tobermory.

Once parked he left her with a brief nod, obviously dismissing her from his mind as easily as he did their barbed conversation, although he did arrange to meet her later for tea.

Tobermory was a beautiful little town on the northeast side of the island, and one of the safest anchorages. The harbour, gracefully shaped, faced east, with steep hill-slopes encircling it and falling to the water's edge. Sara wandered slowly around, enjoying her freedom, feeling totally relaxed after days spent at her typewriter. She found her work interesting, some of old Mr Fraser's documents were totally absorbing, but it was nice to be out.

In such a short space of time the strange tightness which had gripped her heart since her parents' death seemed to ease almost completely. She would never be able to understand why such accidents had to happen, but the sharp, piercing edge of resentment was gently disappearing, and in its place came a less hurtful acceptance of the inevitable. As she stood there, in the warm sunshine, she could feel a new lightness of spirit which she had thought lost for ever.

If only Jane could have been here. She must write and tell her about it. After all, it had been her idea in the first place. She walked on towards the harbour. Inadvertently, because she was thinking of Jane, her thoughts strayed to James Kerr. He had been in love with Jane for years and Mummy used to say it would be an ideal match, but Jane always hesitated. Perhaps she was right when she said that marriage didn't always spell happiness. Ambiguously Sara's thoughts went to Hugh Fraser.

Impatiently she shrugged her slim shoulders. Why did her mind keep edging towards him? She knew that part of herself felt his dark attraction intensely, which wasn't the same as falling in love with him, she told herself firmly. She was only conscious of him because they spent so much time working together. When Jill came and she got out more, things would soon fall into their proper perspective!

Determined to forget about him for a while, she wandered around the harbour, keeping to the main street which followed the harbour wall, looking at the eighteenth-century houses with their pointed attics and different coloured, painted stone walls. Everything looked neat and bright and curiously deserted.

The air of sleepiness was infectious. Completely

submissive, Sara leant over the low harbour wall, the fresh sea air softly caressing her face and gently lifting her neatly combed hair. In the warmth of the sun she felt her eyelids closing.

It was then that some heightened sense of perception caused her to jerk upright and stare across the road. To her surprise the young man who had rescued her bag on the day she had arrived was strolling out of one of the shops along the sea-front. Sara blinked and looked again. It was the same bearded stranger; she would recognize his face anywhere.

While she watched undetected he loaded a box of provisions into the boot of his car. So he was still here! Maybe he was an islander after all? Or he could have rented accommodation where he looked after himself, which would account for the groceries. For no particular reason a curious frown creased Sara's brows as she watched him drive quickly away. He had glanced briefly in her direction, but given no indication that he knew her. Probably this wasn't surprising as their former acquaintance had been short, but somehow she found this difficult to believe. Puzzled, but not unduly perturbed, she turned back to her silent contemplation of the bay.

She told Hugh about him later, on their way home. "I suppose a lot of tourists visit Mull every year?" she finished lamely, wishing rather belatedly that she had never mentioned the man. Hugh probably thought her insatiably curious.

"Do you feel interested in him, Sara?" As he turned the big car he ignored her question by asking one of his own, his voice deliberately smooth as he glanced at her delicate profile.

She refused to be angry. "Not particularly," she said truthfully, "I just wondered why he hadn't

54

moved on."

"Well, don't let it bother you." His hard grin was slightly malicious. "Small communities breed curiosity, remember. Have you ever lived in a small place, Sara?"

She smiled ruefully, remembering the country town she called home, but she also recalled the lack of loneliness, the fun, and the shared interests. "People care in small communities," she said fiercely.

He retorted sharply, "They can be stifling."

"I don't think so!"

"So we must agree to differ," he drawled. "We appear to differ about many things, I believe?"

Sara sensed in his words a certain restiveness. Almost as if he was discovering and disliking a need to come to terms with another way of life. Was he finding the tenacious pull of a more settled existence so very irritating when he enjoyed his freedom and roaming the world? She turned her attention to his last question. "Do you find it surprising that we haven't much in common?"

"Ha!" He threw back his dark head and laughed. "Didn't anyone ever tell you, Sara, that men and women very rarely have much in common, to begin with anyway, and the one emotion which sometimes bridges the gap is extremely hazardous."

"You mean—love?"

His eyes glinted on her hot cheeks and he sounded unbearably cynical. "I do. Have you ever been in love?"

Sara turned her head. Not really, she could have told him, but because she felt he was intentionally treading on holy ground she remained silent. Besides, why should she admit her own inexperience? He was arrogant enough to find it entertaining!

"You'll have to take the plunge some time," he mocked, as she sat inarticulate, "but I wouldn't advise you to choose a passing tourist."

"Have no fear, I won't. I can always wait until I return to London." Just so long as I don't fall for you, her wayward heart prayed as his taunting gaze swung to her face and lingered, as it had done once before, on her vulnerable mouth before returning to the road again. Her pulse raced as if she had been running, almost as if he had taken her physically in his arms and kissed her.

The irony crept back into his face. "Of course," he murmured, "the great metropolis! And you like to pretend you can do without it!" He shrugged his shoulders indifferently, apparently losing interest in their conversation as he concentrated on his driving. Sara felt a curious tension slowly leave her limbs.

They were returning by the east coast to Salen, but for once Sara stared unseeing at the spectacular sea-scapes. Hugh had taken her for tea to the largest hotel in Tobermory, and been attentive enough to satisfy any girl's ego. When he liked he had a charm which she thought might be calculated, but against which she had found she had little defence. Against her will she had found herself responding. The danger lay in allowing herself to be lulled into a state of credulity. In thinking that Lochgoil composed his world, instead of being just a place he would dispose of, along with herself, as soon as it was suitably convenient!

She lay back in her seat and half closed her eyes as they swept around the next bend. "A penny for them?" he smiled idly, confounding her suspicions that his thoughts were elsewhere. Then before she could reply he turned the car sharply into a passing place and jumped out.

There was another car parked there, a long luxurious sports model, and a tall dark girl stood beside it, obviously in trouble. She was surveying it moodily, but as Hugh stopped Sara saw her sullen expression change to one of startled delight.

"Hugh!" she cried gladly, throwing her arms around his neck and holding her red mouth up to be kissed. "I'd no idea you were here!"

Hugh laughed, and Sara watched curiously as he embraced the girl lightly, holding her at arms' length. "It's good to see you again, Beth. I thought you were still in France?" He kissed her again, quite tenderly, Sara thought.

Something clicked in Sara's head as she remembered Biddy saying, on the night she had arrived, that the girl Hugh might marry was in France. Could this be the girl, or was it just a coincidence that she had been in France too?

"I was." Beth's rather deep voice carried. "I just got home yesterday and thought I'd take the car out for a run. I'm afraid it stands in the garage too much. Unfortunately I seem to have a flat tyre, and was hoping someone would come along and fix it for me, but I never expected it would be you!"

Hugh smiled lazily as he bent down to look at the wheel. "I always know when to turn up," he teased. Sara saw his teeth gleam white and hard. With laughter lightening up his face and accentuating the arrogant tilt of his head he looked like some dark pirate, and, Sara suspected, was quite capable of acting like one!

Beth's eyes, Sara noticed, never left his face as she asked quickly where he had been.

"To Tobermory," Hugh waved negligently towards Sara. "With my new secretary, so you're in luck. Sara

57

Winton, Beth Asquith," he introduced them.

"Secretary?" Beth's bewildered eyes turned to where Sara sat in the Jaguar, obviously seeing her for the first time. "What on earth do you want with a secretary at Lochgoil?" Her words penetrated clearly and coldly as she swung back indignantly to Hugh who was already removing his jacket, prior to changing her tyre.

"You'd be surprised," he mocked, his amused glance moving briefly to Sara's face, and she flushed with annoyed confusion before Beth's unfriendly eyes.

Beth must surely realize that he was only teasing, but how dared he even hint of an intimacy which didn't exist! No doubt Beth would find out soon enough that the relationship he alluded to was strictly on a working basis, but she seemed a girl with little sense of humour and it was unkind of Hugh to tease her in such a way. "I could have helped with your office work myself," Sara heard her say.

She didn't hear Hugh's reply, but whatever it was it appeared to satisfy Beth. Her tight expression relaxed as she crouched by his side apparently intent on exchanging gossip.

Sara frowned suddenly. This must be the woman who Biddy had hinted might be Hugh Fraser's future wife. An unaccountable feeling of dismay caught her heart only to be squashed immediately. Beth must be near his own age, and eminently suitable, and it was plan that she was more than a little attracted towards him. A marriage between them might provide exactly the right incentive he needed to settle down on the island, and would probably solve a lot of problems. Sara couldn't think why the idea of it should prove so distasteful.

Next day Jill arrived. For Sara the day started

badly with Katie rousing her before seven, telling her that Biddy had taken to her bed, and that Mr Hugh had told her to get Miss Winton up to cook breakfast.

"It's her pains again, miss," Katie explained when Sara ran quickly downstairs. "Usually when she can't get up I try to manage myself, but last time I scalded my hand with the kettle and burnt the toast, and old Mr Fraser said that he felt poorly all day afterwards. I didn't like to ask you, miss, but Mr Hugh said that you're sure to be a good cook."

And what if I am? Sara thought resentfully, as she knotted herself into one of Biddy's huge white aprons. Surely he didn't expect her to turn her hand to everything? Regarding Biddy's rheumatism, he'd soon be murmuring—"I'm sure with your nursing experience, Sara—"

Sara refused to admit that most of her ill-humour might stem from the night before. When after leaving Beth he had apparently forgotten all about his offer to let her drive the car. Or was it because the afternoon had seemed spoilt when Beth, with a few chilly, well chosen words, had let Sara know quite clearly that she wasn't welcome at Lochgoil? Hugh, busy with Beth's car, probably hadn't heard.

Hastily Sara poured a cup of tea and arranged some biscuits daintily on a rose-patterned plate. "I'll take Biddy's tray up myself," she told a hovering Katie, "before I get breakfast. I might be able to make her more comfortable."

Biddy complained of severe pains in her hip and said that the doctor's tablets didn't agree with her so she had put them down the sink. She seemed pleased with the tea, although she told Sara she shouldn't have bothered.

"I think aspirin's as good as most things." Sara

59

shook two tablets from a bottle which she had found in the kitchen, and surprisingly Biddy swallowed them obediently, while Sara watched and made a mental note to have a word with her doctor. "What you need right now is rest and warmth," she said firmly, as Biddy tried to get up.

"There is another woman in the house besides myself and Miss Jill, who is coming today. Surely we can manage between the lot of us!"

"Miss Jill?" Biddy's sea-washed blue eyes widened with dismay. "Indeed, I almost forgot. What will Mr Hugh say if I'm still in bed?"

"Nothing to what I'll say if you get up!" Sara retorted tartly, as she closed the door.

Now for 'Mr Hugh', she thought crossly, making her way to the kitchen again. Almost certainly Biddy would be up in a day or two, but in the meantime if Hugh intended that she should do the cooking then he would have to manage in the office by himself. She couldn't do both, and it would do him no harm to find out that she wasn't as compliant as he thought.

She found him waiting in the kitchen, standing by the window looking out on to the courtyard, the wide bulk of his shoulders almost filling the long, narrow opening. For a suspended moment a strange excitement held her silent.

He swung around, hearing her footsteps, his eyes flickering across her young flawless face. "Good morning, Sara. I thought it would help if I had breakfast here with you."

How cosy it sounded, if a girl didn't sense the thread of masculine impatience underneath. His smile scarcely concealed the fact that he didn't appreciate this change of routine. Sara nodded coolly as she popped some rashers of bacon under the grill.

"How many eggs do you like?" she asked sharply, reaching for the frying pan.

Hugh's smile broadened with amusement as he came and stood beside her. "We're not in a very good mood this morning, are we?" He glanced down his straight nose at her, his eyes brilliantly mocking. "Are you annoyed with me because I asked you to do this?"

In spite of herself Sara laughed, her anger subsiding. "Not really." Her blue eyes met his, greatly daring. "But you do enjoy giving orders."

"You don't mind helping out, do you, Sara?"

"Not if I'm asked properly." She knew she was being childish, but some streak of perverseness made her go on, even while she was aware that he was baiting her deliberately.

He grinned. "I'm too used to giving orders, Sara. I've almost forgotten how to ask—properly. Perhaps you can teach me?" He still towered over her against the cooker. He had been out riding and smelt faintly, sensually, of good leather and horses. Sara's senses responded traitorously.

"Well, I can't do everything!" Attempting to regain her lost composure, she broke an egg recklessly into the hot fat. "What about the office?"

She didn't win this round either! "I could always ask Beth when she looks in this evening," he said blandly, his eyes on the smooth whiteness of her throat where her shirt lay open at the neck, "She did offer."

Sara spooned fat over the eggs too quickly, and a small gasp of pain escaped her as the hot liquid splashed on her bare arm. She dropped the spoon and snatched her arm, tears of despair clouding her eyes as she tried to cover the burnt patch with her hand.

There was a smothered exclamation from Hugh.

"Here, let me see that!" Tersely he took her hand away and inspected the damage. "I thought Katie was the only careless one around here. How many more times do I have to rescue you, I wonder?" Glancing swiftly at her shocked face, he went to a cupboard and returned with a tube of ointment which he smeared liberally over the burn. It was the second time since it had happened that he had alluded to her accident on the cliffs!

"That's enough," Sara cried sharply, as he emptied the tube. His fingers seemed to burn more than the fat, and she felt defensively shaken. "I'm sorry," she murmured, rather shamefaced, withdrawing her arm. "It's nothing really. I expect I got a fright."

She could smell something burning and moved away from him to rescue the frying pan. "If you like I could work in the office after lunch, after I'm finished here. Katie should be able to manage for an hour or two."

"So we won't need Beth after all," he tacked on, suavely, glancing at her speculatively from narrowed eyes as he searched in the first-aid box for a bandage.

"Not necessarily, but just as you like." Sara's even white teeth caught her bottom lip sharply. She held out her arm obediently while he tied the bandage firmly and expertly, his deft movements speaking of considerable experience. Her arm still hurt, but she felt a slow colour coming back into her cheeks. She didn't know why, but she didn't care for the idea of Beth 'helping out', and had a certain feeling that Hugh guessed. The odd quirk at the side of his mouth proclaimed it.

He gave the bandage a small purposeful twitch. "When you've finished sorting things out in that attractive head of yours, do you think we might have breakfast? A hot cup of tea and a couple of these should see you through." Silently he handed her the aspirin bottle which she had placed on the table herself after coming down from Biddy.

"Thank you," Sara said tonelessly, her voice empty of gratitude. Was he deliberately punishing her for her contrariness? His advice was sound. It was exactly what her father might have given, only he wasn't her father, but a much younger man whom she was becoming increasingly aware of. She was also aware that she was curiously sensitive about his spartan treatment of her arm, in spite of her own protests that the burn was only superficial. And especially after the rather satisfying intensity of his first reactions. He had had much more real sympathy with Beth and her flat tyre! Resentfully she turned to lay the table.

Determinedly she allowed herself no time to sulk. After breakfast she kept busy and out of Hugh's way. While she prepared lunch she pondered on the intricacies of working in a private household. It bred a certain intimacy one didn't find in an ordinary office, which might be dangerous if she couldn't keep her involvement on an impersonal level. It grew increasingly difficult to think of Hugh strictly as her boss. Her inclination earlier this morning to bury her head against his shoulder had been wholly disconcerting! Perhaps it was just as well that his momentary concern had turned to indifference.

Some time later she managed to contact the family doctor on the telephone—Ian McKenzie. After much searching she found his number on an old card index in a cupboard in the hall. She must remember to ask Hugh about a proper directory. So far she hadn't seen one.

Tentatively she rang the surgery and managed to

speak to the doctor himself. Yes, he would pop in and see Biddy later, and bring some more tablets.

"It's often a question of trial and error," he sighed, when she mentioned the fate of Biddy's previous supply. And when she had rather timidly suggested that bed might be the best treatment, he had snorted loudly, "Just you try keeping her there!" and rung off.

It just wasn't her day, Sara decided wryly, as she helped Katie prepare Jill's room. Katie confided that her boy-friend wasn't coming to see her that weekend.

"I'm getting tired of him, anyway," she said crossly, dusting the furniture with unnecessary vigour until the wood gleamed. "He's working on the mainland in one of the hotels, and they're so busy he can hardly get away. If he's not careful I'll be looking for somebody else!"

The hidden threat in her voice made Sara smile as she gave the satin bedspread a final flick. It didn't seem to be Katie's day either, but the knowledge brought no consolation, only a mounting despair.

CHAPTER FOUR

SHORTLY after lunch Hugh went to Salen to meet his stepsister off the plane. Sara was in her room later in the afternoon when she heard a quick knock on her door, and without waiting to be invited a small fair girl with a gay, vivacious smile wandered in.

Her eyebrows were question marks as she said lightly. "I believe you're Hugh's new secretary? I thought I'd come and look you over." She broke off abruptly to stare wide-eyed at Sara. "I must say I didn't expect to see anyone quite like you! Wherever did he find you?"

"He didn't, actually. I was sent," Sara replied evenly, shooting the girl a quick glance as she put down her hairbrush. She realized instinctively that this was Jill, although she in no way resembled her brother, apart from possibly sharing his arrogance. That strange mixture of arrogance and familiarity which could be so confusing, but proclaimed more than anything else could have done that she was a member of this particular branch of the Fraser family. She waited in silence as Jill obviously pondered on what she had said.

"Sent?" The girl's light voice sharpened with curiosity as she noted Sara's slender good looks. "What on earth do you mean by that? Who sent you?"

Sara blinked, startled by the almost unfriendly tone of Jill's voice. It took her all her time to keep back an equally sharp retort. Somehow she had a feeling that in spite of her manner, Jill wasn't being intentionally rude. She struck Sara, in that instant, as being very much on the defensive, and trying to hide it. Her brown eyes, as she watched Sara, held a certain wariness, a hint of suspicion which was not easily concealed. Surely Hugh hadn't said anything to antagonize his sister at this early stage? But it might be better to tread carefully.

Rather vaguely, she smiled. "Mr Fraser asked his solicitor to send him a secretary—so I'm here."

"Oh, I see." Jill's expression said quite clearly that she didn't. It was still dubious as for a brief second she contemplated Sara's smooth complexion. Then suddenly, as if deciding to change her tactics, she held out her hand. "I'm Jill," she explained, somewhat unnecessarily. "And I'm sorry if I've seemed a bit rude. But you can blame Hugh. He never explains anything properly, and always rubs me up the wrong way."

So he had been saying something! Sara frowned. "I'm afraid I'm not with you?" Deliberately she phrased her question lightly, concealing a stab of dismay.

Jill took her time, smiling complacently, rather like a cat as she curled herself snugly into Sara's armchair. Obviously she sensed Sara's discomfort and, perversely, was in no hurry to alleviate it. "He's been telling me," she smiled, "that you're here partly for my benefit. So out of character that he should consider little me. Why should he suddenly consider that I need a keeper? Or a nursemaid? Can you wonder if I'm suspicious? Certainly there's no reason why he should put himself out for me!"

"I'm afraid you've got me all wrong." Somewhat relieved, Sara sat down on the end of her bed. Jill was certainly mixed up, although it might have been better

66

if Hugh had said nothing at all. A twinge of irritation replaced her former dismay. Men very rarely appeared to display much finesse when dealing with a younger sister. "I'm actually here to help clear up your uncle's estate, and I only expect to be here for a few weeks. So I don't think that you have much to worry about."

Contrary to what she had hoped, Jill wasn't so easily put off. Her eyes narrowed with a surprising shrewdness. "Your motives might be clear," she frowned, "but how about Hugh?"

Sara hesitated, just slightly. So far Jill had made no reference whatsoever to the boy-friend whom Hugh was alarmed about, but it did seem obvious that he was on her mind. Well, Sara had no intention of getting involved in any family disputes if she could help it, and unless Jill asked specifically, didn't intend mentioning him herself. Fortunately Hugh wouldn't want her to either, as it was only with comparative secrecy that his plan could hope to succeed. Feeling rather ashamed of her own astuteness, Sara replied more warmly than she might otherwise have done.

"Don't you think that you're making a bit much of this, Jill? Mr Fraser did tell me that he feels a certain responsibility, especially when you've been ill, and, I suppose, because your mother's in America."

"And when she returns he'll hand me back like a parcel, all neatly labelled and undamaged! Poor Hugh. I guess I get the picture." Jill laughed derisively, her brown eyes flashing. "I'm afraid he hates encumbrances of any kind. Mummy always says this is why he never married. That his conscience wouldn't allow him to roam the world and leave his poor little wife at home!"

Sara jumped uncomfortably to her feet. aware that Jill watched her closely, as if still not completely satisfied. Jill was crafty! She might be spoilt, but basically she was sensible enough. She seemed to know what she was after. Sara didn't. Like her brother Jill appeared to employ devious methods, and Sara instinctively felt that at the moment, her best form of defence was to retreat.

"I must fly!" she exclaimed, glancing swiftly at her watch. "If you will excuse me. I almost forgot about Biddy. She's ill in bed, and I must go and see how she is."

"Oh, that reminds me . . ." Jill yawned as she unwound herself lazily from the chair and stretched her arms. "Hugh did tell me that Doctor McKenzie would like to see you. That's actually why I'm here."

Half-way through the door Sara stopped. Turning her gleaming head, she threw Jill an exasperated look. "You could have told me sooner!"

"Sorry, I forgot." Still indifferent, Jill shrugged. "But don't worry. He's an old dear. I'm sure he won't mind being kept waiting, especially by a girl who looks like you."

Without waiting to hear more, Sara fled and sped downstairs. She knew all about doctors being old dears! They were just as often overworked and grumpy, and objected to being kept hanging around. More than likely he had gone by now, and she had wanted to talk to him about Biddy.

To her surprise Hugh was in the hall, standing talking to a younger man. Probably a neighbour? And to her dismay she could see no sign of any doctor.

Hugh turned as she walked towards them over the thick carpet, his dark eyes slanting to her anxious face, a faint smile edging his firm mouth. "I think you'd better meet Doctor McKenzie, Sara, as you seem to have taken charge of Biddy."

68

Sara might have managed a dry retort if she hadn't felt so silly. It had just been a figure of speech, she supposed, as she shook hands. Unless Ian McKenzie really did seem old to Jill. Somehow, she doubted it. The doctor was not handsome, but his face had a certain charm, a homespun attraction all of its own. He was younger than Hugh, and, like herself, very fair.

She sensed in his regard a quickening interest. There was nothing subtle about his admiration. It was clearly to be seen in his grey eyes.

"So you're the young lady who intends keeping Biddy in bed," he smiled, retaining his firm grip on her slim fingers, his eyes fixed on her flushed cheeks.

That Dr McKenzie was acting somewhat out of character Sara had no means of knowing, but she did know that she found his obvious appreciation stimulating after a particularly tedious morning. Femininely ignoring Hugh's slight frown, a responsive smile curved her lips.

"I'm going to try." Carefully she extricated her fingers, as she asked if he had left any tablets. "Biddy couldn't remember just what you've been giving her."

"I've got some in the car, if you'd like to come with me and get them." Ian didn't take his eyes from Sara's face. "If you can persuade her to take them and stay in bed, so much the better."

"I'll try," Sara repeated, suddenly very much aware of Hugh in the background watching them cynically. She pretended an indifference she didn't feel as she smiled again at the doctor. She wasn't a stranger to his intolerance, but was dismayed that it was beginning to hurt.

She was surprised, and not a little annoyed, when he intervened dryly, "As you're obviously not in a hurry, Ian, you might take a look at Sara's arm before you go. She spilt some hot fat on it this morning. I'm afraid she's not always as efficient as she seems."

Sara's eyes flew open wrathfully as she met his sardonic gaze. Her arm did hurt, but not that much! Foolishly she wished he hadn't mentioned it. She dragged her eyes away from his, smiling at Ian, trying a little desperately to regain a sense of balance.

"I don't think you should bother," she protested, as Ian made to remove the bandage. She disregarded his sudden frown. "I had a look at it myself after lunch and it's quite all right."

"How do you know?" Ian's frown deepened impatiently. "Have you had any nursing experience? Even a small burn can be nasty."

"But I've seen dozens!" Stung by the reproving note in his voice, Sara allowed her agitation to run away with discretion. "I used to help my father. He was a doctor, too."

Half reassured, Ian let go of her arm, although his reluctance was obvious. "Well, just as you like." His keen eyes dwelt on her consideringly. "All the same, while we're seeking Biddy's tablets I'll give you something you might like to try. At least it can't do any harm." With a brief word of farewell to Hugh he guided her out through the door.

When she returned, ten minutes later, Hugh was gone, and she could see no sign of him in the library when she went to see if he needed any immediate help. Ian had insisted that she had a proper dressing on her arm, and this had taken time. And Sara didn't care to admit, even to herself, that she had lingered with Ian deliberately, hoping to avoid Hugh and any caustic remarks he might make about her behaviour when she got back.

For the remainder of the afternoon Jill plagued her

in the kitchen, already complaining of being bored. She laughed with Katie whom she knew well, and teased Sara about Ian McKenzie.

"I saw you holding hands in the hall. What were you discussing so earnestly? Surely not Biddy's arthritis? I told Hugh afterwards that Ian seemed quite smitten."

Sara sighed, glancing at Jill's mischievous face, thankful that Katie was in the larder. "You told me that Doctor McKenzie was an old dear." Heavily she emphasized the last two words.

Jill giggled unrepentantly. "Well, isn't he? Uncle David used to say he was born old—old and overbearing. All he ever prescribed for me was a lecture!"

Sara tried unsuccessfully to conceal a grin as she bent to pop a casserole into the oven. Perhaps it wasn't Jill's fault that she seemed much younger than she actually was. She was amusing, but her inconsequential chatter might get wearisome. It might be better not to mention that Ian had asked her out with him to a party. A *ceilidh*, he had called it. With so much to do here, she hadn't felt free to accept, but neither had she turned him down. She had promised to let him know some time in the next week or so.

"When does your mother return from America?" she asked, veering away from Ian as she untied her apron prior to changing for dinner. Katie could manage now. The casserole was easy. She would bring it to the table and they could all help themselves. Sara was not really interested in Mrs Fraser as she didn't know her, but she might be a safer topic than Ian McKenzie.

Jill was diverted, although not happily. "I don't really know," she shrugged vaguely, following Sara across the hall. "One of these days, I suppose."

71

"You didn't go with her?"

"Obviously not!" Jill's lips curled petulantly. "I might have done, but she wouldn't wait until I'd had this operation."

Sara bit her bottom lip doubtfully. If Jill had been keen to go to America, then surely she couldn't be seriously in love with a man in London. Unless she had intended taking him with her?

Jill continued when Sara made no comment, her voice still peevish, "I have an odd feeling that Mummy deliberately went when she knew I couldn't go with her. Personal family reasons, she said, whatever they add up to? All very hush-hush, but I'm sure Hugh knows! Perhaps you could wheedle it out of him for me?"

Wheedle it out of him! Sara paused by her bedroom door and almost laughed. No one would get anything out of him by devious methods or otherwise, and she wouldn't like to try. And certainly not to appease Jill's curiosity. "I'll leave that to you," she smiled, as she gently closed the door.

After dinner she went with Hugh to the library. There were one or two things to clear up, he said, some correspondence which must be seen to. She could type it out tomorrow in her own time, so long as it caught the afternoon post.

Immaculately dressed in a grey lounge suit, he looked lean and attractive. Sara nodded as she sat down, and for a while they worked almost in silence, the deep inflection of his voice as he dictated letters playing oddly on her nerves.

When he finished he reached for a cigarette and after lighting it blew the smoke hard through his nostrils. At that moment he looked like some ruthless tycoon, willing and able to put anyone's head on the block. Sara held her breath as her eyes slipped from his teak-carved face and looked away, seeking for something to distract her attention.

Inadvertently she caught her own reflection in the long mirror by the fireplace, and studied herself objectively. The pale blouse she wore with her long black velvet skirt seemed to emphasize her slimness and enhance her air of fragility. Her hair, tonight, looked very fair and beautiful. Suddenly, irrelevantly, she was pleased that she wasn't exactly ugly.

She glanced back at the room and felt her cheeks go pink as she intercepted Hugh's sardonic gaze. Obviously he thought her foolish, and she couldn't really blame him. There was something faintly ludicrous about staring at oneself in a mirror. She supposed he thought her a silly vain creature. Not that she ever knew what he was thinking. His real thoughts were so often cloaked by a teasing ambiguity.

He surprised—and embarrassed—her by saying lightly, "You look beautiful, and your dinner was delicious. I don't know how you manage it. At any rate my intuition about your cooking has proved correct."

"And if it hadn't?"

He grinned. "We do observe a modicum of politeness, even in these uncivilized parts."

"You surprise me."

He shrugged off her irony. "Biddy seems comfortable and my sister hasn't complained. At times I must admit your competence surprises me."

She looked back at him defiantly, willing herself not to weaken. "You shouldn't prejudge people."

"I don't."

"But you did me?" She was alarmed by her own daring.

He paused, his eyes running smoothly over her. "I'll

73

confess," he said suavely, "that you seemed a shade ornamental for my purpose, and possibly too young."

"Competence and a pleasant appearance often go together," she countered, inwardly annoyed by his bluntness.

"There are different kinds of attractiveness. A man needs to retain his peace of mind."

She made an effort to stay cool, and looked away from the mild derisiveness of his dark eyes. It was her own fault, she shouldn't have tried to provoke him. What hope had any girl of penetrating his cast-iron equilibrium? She tried to ignore the subtle taunts in his voice.

"Competence isn't just the prerogative of age," she persisted stubbornly, "as you must know."

"Women know most of the answers before they leave the cradle." His eyes glittered with cool amusement. "Whereas men get off to a bad start. Take Ian McKenzie, for instance. Completely knocked sideways by one glance from your forget-me-not blue eyes, in spite of the fact that you had kept him waiting."

Sara glanced at him quickly, a little shamefaced. "I was sorry about that," she murmured, looking down at her hands. "I was talking to Jill and forgot about the time."

Somehow she was reluctant to explain that Jill had forgotten to give her the message until the last moment. Much better to let him think that she had been careless herself, rather than risk antagonizing his already tense relationship with his sister.

But it was certainly her own fault that she had omitted to apologize to Ian. Her surprise at his comparatively youthful appearance had put this right out of her mind, but again she felt that such an explanation would sound foolish.

She contented herself by adding quietly, "Dr McKenzie did explain several things about Biddy's condition when we went to get her tablets from his car." She ignored his caustic remark about Ian being knocked sideways.

"All very proper, Miss Winton," he said smoothly, getting slowly to his feet, smiling softly. "I do beg your pardon!"

Sara flushed, not looking at his sceptical face as she scrambled to her own feet, saying swiftly, "If we're quite finished here, I'm going for a breath of fresh air. Jill went to bed early, I heard her go upstairs some time ago, and Biddy's all right. I'll take her a hot drink when I get back."

She moved towards the door and he turned quickly by her side, switching off the lights as they went out.

"If you don't mind, I'll come with you." His clipped voice halted her abruptly. The moon was full and Sara had always liked to wander on her own. She didn't want him with her. She wanted to relax. Her eyes met his a little desperately.

"If you don't mind, I'd rather go by myself. It's not late."

His cool stare hardened as his hand fell from the light switch. "I'm afraid I do mind. And it might be safer—rescuing you in daylight was bad enough. Besides, I feel like a walk myself, and there are still things I want to discuss. Tomorrow I have to go to London, so there won't be time."

How could she refuse? Without further protest she found a light wrap and slipped it around her shoulders. She should be warm enough without a proper coat as she didn't intend going far.

The stars were very bright in an almost cloudless

sky and a light wind was rising. The castle looked mythical flooded in starlight, and the sea behind it drenched in silver as the moving water caught the light from the moon. It was a lovely sight, she thought wistfully, as she followed Hugh down to the beach.

Sara went quickly, as if reluctant to prolong such a moment, intensely aware of the man by her side. They went by the way he had shown her before, but every so often she found herself having to pause, having little struggles with her hair, as the wind blew silky strands across her eyes and mouth. She clicked her tongue in exasperation as Hugh walked ahead. Her hair and her long clinging skirt hindered and she hurried to catch him up.

"Are we in a race?" She couldn't keep the impatience from her voice as she stumbled on a rough patch of seaweed. Perversely, now that she was out, she wanted to linger, to enjoy the sight and sound of the waves breaking against the shore, but he went too quickly.

He stopped suddenly and gave a low laugh. Her pulse jerked as she felt him take her hand and twine his fingers lazily through hers. They were lean and strong and did peculiar things to her poise. Something inside her began to stir and stretch, slowly unfurling, something entirely new and not a little alarming. His touch brought a burning sensation to her throat, and her whole body ached with a curious longing.

A night owl somewhere on the cliffs gave a lonely cry. Sara caught the warning note of its call although she scarcely heard it.

At once they were on smoother ground and he released her fingers, and she prayed fervently that he had not felt their convulsive trembling. He didn't have to know the tumultuous reaction of her heart. His hand had gone out as it might have done to a child. Her own vivid response had been purely physical, a trick of the night.

Unable to face a more stringent self-analysis, she swung around to face him, uttering the first thing that came into her head. "When will you return from London?"

The deep silence endued her words with a breathless quality. She was immediately sorry she had asked.

He stopped, his hand going out to twist a wayward strand of hair around her throat, revealing the pure grace of line from forehead to chin. "Are you glad I'm going, Sara?" His voice backed on an enigmatical note, as he probed her eyes in the darkness.

She tried to imitate his cool sophistication, knowing clearly that she was no match for his verbal expertise. She remembered once he had mocked her inability to retaliate. She would concede this, but not completely!

"You did say that while you were gone I might have a holiday," she quoted deliberately.

His teeth gleamed white. "And you choose to remind me of it when you've just taken on the role of cook-housekeeper! If I recall rightly there was a proviso."

"A proviso?"

"You promised to keep an eye on Jill."

"Not voluntarily."

He ignored this. "The added responsibility will help you grow up—or don't you want to?"

She refused to explore the unfairness of this. "I don't need to grow up. I'm twenty-one. Or didn't you know?"

"So old!" he laughed, but this time without amusement, his eyes on her star-flecked face. "Age isn't necessarily defined by years," he said dryly.

"Experience, you mean?" She breathed the word nervously, drawing away from him.

"You could say that. Something a bit beyond you, I imagine." He flung the ball straight back into her court.

She shivered, but he continued unmercifully, "You've been too tied to apron strings to get much of that."

Sara stared back into his dark handsome face, her hair spilling like silk over her shoulders, blending with the moonlight. "So you've checked me!"

He leaned towards her, his expression inscrutable. "My dear girl, I didn't need to. One only needs to look at you."

Her voice thinned on a note of fury. "You're impossible!"

"So are you," he retorted suavely. "Let's call a truce."

She bit her lip hard, making a visible effort not to quarrel with him fiercely. She couldn't remember being roused like this before. Removing herself a few steps from his too close proximity, she stooped and picked a pebble from beneath her feet and flung it with feeling to where the waves were breaking softly on the shore.

After the faint plop she breathed more freely and spoke again. "What do you want me to do with Jill while you're away. She hasn't mentioned any boyfriend. Are you sure she's got one?"

He replied sharply, obviously not welcoming this particular change of subject, "I can assure you he still exists. We had quite an argument about him coming from the air-strip."

She traced a ribbon of moonlight across the sand, her profile delicately outlined against the fluorescent

78

glow. "Opposition often has an adverse effect."

"Do you really want to talk about Jill?"

The dry sand trickled through the open toes of her sandals, curiously pagan. The scent from the sea invaded the senses, permeating the air with a kind of magic, as it drifted in with the tide. Desire stirred. It was not a night for logical thinking, but she made a determined effort.

"I thought this was why you came with me?"

His dark brows slanted upwards, giving him, in the half-light, a faintly saturnine look. All around them shadows loomed. Inky green shadows, black patches from the rock, a white cloud across the moon casting pools of darkness on to the beach.

"A night like this wasn't meant for discussion," he said, softly derisive.

She tensed, poised like a slender sea nymph ready for flight, her head thrown back on a slender neck, eyes dilated. She knew a curious timeless sensation, as she swallowed dryly. "I don't think I understand?"

His eyes glittered, a long deliberate speculation, "You don't think that it's time you did?"

Did a hint of a threat lie hidden in that one brief question? His dark mocking face swam in front of her. How easy—and how dangerous—to fall under the potent charm of this man. "I don't have to listen to this," she said weakly, flinching against the appraisal of his narrowed eyes.

He laughed deep in his throat. "I don't propose acting the primitive savage, if that's what you're afraid of?"

Sara quivered as his hand went out again to her hair, twisting a coil of it around his fingers, silver in the moonlight. He went on, tautly, on the same theme, "But I can't help wondering how you'd react if I did.

Is that innocent aura of yours just skin deep, I wonder? When girls like you choose to bury themselves on a remote island it's usually because of a man!"

She couldn't control a nervous tremor. His hand against her nape sent a thousand sensations down her spine, swamping clear thinking. "You don't know why I really came?"

"I thought it might be interesting to find out, after seeing the way you looked at Ian McKenzie," He sounded unbearably cynical.

"How dare you!" Her anger flared, only to die as quickly. She brushed the back of her hand, a bemused gesture, across her forehead. "Suppose I told you I was unhappy?"

"Spare me the unfortunate details. Mine isn't a shoulder to cry on!"

"No one in their right mind would assume it was!" Unbearably hurt, she hit back wildly, her eyes full of unshed tears, bitterly regretting her impulse to confide. She moved her head impatiently so that her hair swung heavily across her damp face, but already he had caught the betraying glitter in her eyes.

"So help me!" His jaw clamped tight. "Spare me the tears. I promise you that if you cry I shall fly into a volcanic rage! Or perhaps," his voice dropped silkily as his hands tightened over her shoulders, "perhaps I should provide you with something to cry about!"

Sara felt as though her body was suspended in a state of limbo, rising and falling with the tumult of her emotions. One of his hands slid from her shoulder to her waist, dragging her roughly against him. He seemed to act without thinking, the need to punish her for those tears uppermost in his mind as he felt the soft weakness of her body close to his own. She tried to pull away from him, but her body refused to obey the frantic signals from her brain. A silken swathe of hair brushed against his face, igniting a flame as he swept it back with ruthless fingers, and with a groan bent his head and put his mouth to the pale skin of her neck.

Sara, only aware of his anger, felt the hard possessiveness of his lips with a sense of shock, and then his mouth against her neck sent all coherent thoughts out of her mind. She yielded completely, and Hugh only needed to turn his head until his lips found hers.

Sara had been kissed many times before, but never like this. The boys she had known had not been men. In a small town, where she had known most of the boys since childhood, her romances had been light-hearted affairs. She had never been able to respond deeply. Not that she had worried, she had just decided that she wasn't the type. Not frigid exactly, but cool, very cool.

Now she knew different! How naïve she had been. When Hugh kissed her, holding her close against his hard body, she could feel the vivid response of her own. The hard, ruthless pressure of his mouth hurt hers and seemed to possess her utterly, so that her arms slid around his neck convulsively, and she responded without any thought of denial. Her fingers tangled themselves in the thick vitality of his hair, pressing him closer. Time stood still, there was no sound other than the blood beating madly in her ears. She wanted the moment to go on for ever, to keep holding him and never to let him go.

Suddenly, so that the shock of his rejection caught her unawares, he wrenched her arms from around his neck and thrust her firmly away from him.

His voice was harsh. "For a girl without experience you don't do too badly!"

His words were like a douche of cold water. Sara came to her senses. She must be crazy allowing him to treat her like this. "What made you do it?" she asked fiercely between small clenched teeth.

He shrugged, staring at her flushed face in the moonlight. "God knows. Temptation, provocation." His eyes dropped the length of her slender body with disturbing appraisal. "I shouldn't have come down to the beach."

The touch of the breeze was cooling her burning skin. She bit her lips hard where they still smarted from his kisses. "I didn't encourage you!" The statement cloaked her desperate need of reassurance. A negative answer.

He had control of himself again, his face a teak mask. "There are different ways of encouraging a man, Sara. You do it unconsciously all the time."

Dear heavens, how could he say such a thing! Was he trying to make her out a modern Circe? Had she really invited his lovemaking? She refused to believe it.

She stifled a gasp, pressing a hand to her mouth. "That's a horrible thing to say!"

"It's the truth, Sara, whether you're aware of it or not. You attract men like moths to a flame."

She was aghast. Did he think that she was used to such a thing? "I think you've made a mistake—" she began.

"No, I haven't," he retorted forcefully, his voice cooling perceptibly. "But it's late, and you're tired, and we don't want to start something we can't finish." His hand lifted and turned her shoulder gently. "We'll go back. As I said before, I shouldn't have come with you."

"But you said there were things you wanted to

discuss?" She scarcely knew what she was saying, her mind still reeled with shock, and she quivered afresh as she felt the pressure of his guiding fingers through the thin material of her blouse.

His hands dropped to his side as he released her and picked up her wrap. He shrugged, not looking at her. "Nothing that couldn't have waited."

Pulling her wrap close about her, she gave an indifferent movement of her shoulders and stared out to sea. The moon was behind a cloud and she could barely see where she was going. She stumbled and immediately his hand was beneath her elbow, but his touch now was impersonal as he helped her none too kindly up the narrow shadowed track from the beach.

Already she knew that he regretted having held her in his arms. He had used a charm which she had little claim to as an excuse for a moment of weakness. A man, a girl, and a moon. The ingredients had all been there, and he had mixed them. It was as simple as that.

Making a desperate, almost visible effort, to pull herself together, she walked on without replying.

Hugh checked his stride beside her, his dark face inscrutable. His drawl was infinitely mocking. "You don't have to close up on me because I happen to be your employer. You make a habit of referring to your position—a fixed idea in that lovely, old-fashioned head of yours. Girls have been known to marry their boss."

Unaccountably, Sara felt chilled. He was making it sound amusing. She might have forgiven his indifference, but not his ridicule. Swallowing her fury, she said stiffly, "I haven't had many employers, Mr Fraser."

Even to her own ears, the way she spoke his name in that moment sounded incongruous. His fingers hurt again as he stopped abruptly and swung her around. "From now on, my little spitfire," he said, "you can call me Hugh. If you've learnt nothing more salutary from our small skirmish, let it be that."

Sara shivered. Obviously her formality annoyed him, but better that than he should guess the aching response of her body to his compelling embrace. It was as well that he was going away. By the time he returned she might have learned to cope with the jumble of emotions within her, even to assuming a detachment she did not feel.

The castle loomed darkly. Somewhere amongst the trees a bird called, and a tremor ran through her as her gaze travelled from Hugh's sardonic face to the windy sky above them. She was aware of herself as a woman as never before. She was also determined that he shouldn't know it.

She took a deep breath and looked away so that he should not see the tears that stung her eyes. "I think I'd better go," she said stiltedly, pulling herself free of his detaining hands. "I promised Biddy a drink and she'll wonder where I've got to." Turning, she walked quickly away from him through the huge front door.

CHAPTER FIVE

HUGH left early the following day for London. Sara, annoyed because she had overslept after a restless night, ran downstairs to find that he had already had breakfast and gone out. Relief mingled strangely with despair as she stared at his empty chair.

"He was in an awful hurry, miss," Katie spoke with relish behind her. "He said you must be tired, and not to wake you, and wouldn't wait for bacon and eggs. I've just taken Biddy some tea and she's talking of getting up and starting work."

"Oh, no!" With a positive gasp of dismay Sara flew back upstairs to reprimand the wayward Biddy. And by the time she had persuaded her to remain in bed there were several things needing her immediate attention, leaving her no time to snatch more than a cup of coffee and a piece of toast herself.

"Miss Jill's feeling tired," Katie remarked as she carefully prepared a tray. "She says she isn't coming down before lunch."

Sara didn't mind. It would give her time to finish Hugh's letters and he could sign them before he went.

When she did see him he didn't seem at all worried about Jill's fatigue.

"It's only to be expected, I suppose," he said crisply. "The journey here must have tired her, and it will probably take her several days to get over it. I can't see her being much of a nuisance before I get back."

Obviously he wasn't going to commiserate! Without wasting more time he signed the letters and dealt swiftly with the morning's mail.

"I'll be off shortly," he remarked, rapidly clearing the top of his desk before glancing consideringly at Sara's pale face. "I expect you'll cope very well, but in case any sort of emergency should blow up I'll leave you my office number. I'll leave the one for my flat as well, so you should have no difficulty in contacting me."

Sara stared moodily at the top of his dark head as he bent to jot down the telephone numbers. He had changed into a neat town suit, and the colours of the modern striped shirt he wore with it were clean and cool, accentuating his dark masculinity. A pulse beat spasmodically in her throat as she remembered things which were better forgotten, and she forced her eyes away from his enigmatic face.

He straightened, his gaze drifting over her slowly, coming to rest on the neat patch of plaster on her arm. A slightly mocking smile touched the corners of his mouth. "No doubt Dr McKenzie will be keeping an eye on that." He touched the patch lightly with one taunting finger. "Don't fall for him too hard, Sara."

She moved her arm abruptly, ignoring what he said. She tried to pretend indifference, but his remark hurt. "You'll probably be back before he is," she replied.

She looked up and found his eyes narrowed upon her, and for a brief moment was hypnotized by their dark penetration. Rigidly she tried to keep her mind on the few details still to be cleared up, refusing to let it wander back to the evening before. Even so she felt the pink colour stain her cheeks as she hastily gathered together the bundles of correspondence.

He said slowly, deliberately, she thought, "I doubt it. My guess is that you will be seeing him today. In my job I've learnt to assess men and situations. Men like McKenzie aren't easily impressed, but when they are wild horses couldn't stop them."

Did his words hold a subtle note of warning? Clearly he intended that she should be aware of Ian's intentions—if he had any! But surely he wasn't her keeper? Ian had, at least, been consistently courteous, while Hugh could be nice one minute and utterly disparaging the next.

Stung by the mockery in his eyes, she retorted rashly, "You seemed very impressed yourself the other day, with Miss Asquith and her flat tyre!"

His withdrawal was immediate, a physical detachment of his mind from hers. Sara's palms were suddenly moist as she realized the enormity of her indiscretion. But when he spoke again his voice was even, although the mockery still lingered.

"Perhaps it's a case of the morning after the night before, for both of us." He shrugged lightly. It was the only reference he made to their walk on the beach, and she flushed wildly.

For a moment Hugh considered the wild rose colour in her cheeks as she tipped back her shining head and stared at him. His face was very close and she averted her own again.

"I'm sorry," she apologized helplessly above her heartbeats, without being wholly aware of what she was saying.

His eyes glinted with unfathomable humour as he gently flicked her hot cheek before turning abruptly. "I'll see you when I get back," he said quietly over his shoulder, as he strode through the door.

Unable to settle in the house after lunch, Sara decided to go down to the village to post her letters. Biddy required a few things, and had also asked if she would go and see her sister. Biddy had been going to visit her sister that afternoon, but as it was now impossible for her to go, Sara had promised to see if her sister would come to the castle for an hour or two.

She felt a sense of relief to get away from the castle, which seemed strangely empty now that Hugh had gone. Jill hadn't come downstairs until after he left, and then spent the remainder of the morning wandering restlessly from room to room. Sara did suggest that she came with her to Salen, but to her surprise she refused.

"I just can't be bothered," she said, frankly yawning, her small pink mouth petulant. "I'd only be bored. You'll enjoy yourself better without me."

Sara might have said that she wasn't exactly going on a pleasure trip, and that a run out sometimes cheered one up, but she felt it more discreet to say nothing. Obviously, for reasons known only to herself, Jill was in a bad mood, and shrugged off Sara's suggestion that she would feel better as her health improved.

"I'm not an invalid," she insisted crossly, seemingly irritated by Sara's cheerfulness.

Sara smiled, although reluctantly. Jill she felt was easily antagonized, but if they were to live together for the next few weeks it would be pleasanter to remain on good terms. She left her playing records too loudly on her stereo and ran out to get the car.

She approached the Jaguar cautiously. Hugh had told her that morning to take it providing she went carefully.

"It's just a matter of common sense," he had said impatiently, when she protested that she hadn't yet driven it.

Now she hoped fervently that he was right as she reversed the big car cautiously from the garage. In spite of his tolerance she could imagine his withering remarks if she had an accident and did any damage. They might be worse, she thought, than those which he might have made when she mentioned Beth Asquith. His restraint had been remarkable, considering the normal sharpness of his tongue.

As she drove along she wondered unhappily if Beth had gone to London with him, then told herself firmly that it was none of her business. There was no reason at all why they shouldn't go to London together, especially if they were thinking of getting married. Nor was there any logical reason why she should feel so depressed herself at the thought of it. Resolutely she tried to keep her mind on the road.

In Salen Sara quickly posted the letters and purchased the one or two items on Biddy's list. After stowing everything away in the boot of the car she decided to have a look for Biddy's sister. Biddy hadn't been very explicit. She had told Sara to look for a small house on the far side of the town. "Anyone would tell you," she had said.

But Sara couldn't see anyone to ask, and felt cross with herself for not inquiring at the post office. Biddy had given her the name of the house, so not being in any particular hurry she started to explore. It was a fine afternoon, and such an errand would provide an excuse to have a look around. If she didn't find Crag Cottage very soon, she would be surprised.

Then suddenly, around the next corner, she saw Katie, talking to the man with the beard. They were standing close together, half concealed by trees, and deep in conversation.

Sara came to a startled halt and stared. She seemed

destined to bump into him—first in Tobermory, and now here. The surprise this time was finding him talking to Katie. He must surely be one of the islanders? He could even be Katie's boy-friend, although Katie had said that her boy-friend was away from home. On the other hand he might just be passing through and asking Katie the way. There could be many explanations.

Losing interest, Sara turned away to continue her search. She found Miss Black, Biddy's sister, at the other end of the village, and after explaining who she was, waited while the woman put on her best coat and hat.

"Nothing but the best will do for the Castle," Miss Black said cryptically, as she settled down beside Sara. "I remember old Mr Fraser saying that when he first came here. Later he said it about the island. I'm wondering if the young Mr Fraser will be thinking the same way."

Sara knew that she was referring to Hugh, and probably curious, as they all were, to know if he intended to make Lochgoil his home. With her bright, rather bird-like appearance, Miss Black's disappointment was almost tangible as Sara murmured unhelpfully that she had no idea. She might have added with a sigh, that she wished he would make up his mind. Perhaps it gave him a feeling of importance to keep so many people in suspense, patiently waiting his decision, but it certainly wasn't doing anything for his secretary!

Trying to avoid her uneasy thoughts, Sara started chatting about Biddy, and was glad to find Miss Black easily diverted. "I hope she'll feel better in a day or two," she said.

Miss Black sniffed impatiently. "I've told her it's

high time she retired. Not that she's killed with age, mind you, but her pains will get the better of her if she's not careful."

Once started there was no stopping her, and Sara let her talk on, listening with scant attention as her thoughts kept returning to Katie and the stranger.

"Katie's your niece, I believe?" she remarked swiftly, when fortuitously Miss Black made a remark about the girl. She didn't know why she asked the question, but suddenly it seemed important.

"Not niece, exactly," Miss Black explained. "A sort of a cousin a few times removed would be more like it. And she was lucky to get a job at the castle when she didn't go to work on the mainland."

"Why not? I mean . . ." Sara hesitated, not wishing to offend by appearing over-curious, "it must be quiet here for a young girl like Katie?"

"Yes, in a way." Miss Black, just getting into her stride, didn't seem to think there was anything un-usual about Sara's query. "For most young people it it is a bit quiet, although it's probably the shortage of jobs which is the real problem. But you see, Katie's mother died when Katie was a baby, and Katie was left with Biddy and me. She spent a lot of time at the castle when she was a wee girl, and played with Miss Jill whenever she was there on holiday. I suppose you might say they grew up together, though their circum-stances were different, if you know what I mean? Even now the two of them are as thick as thieves, and this was one of the reasons why Katie went to work there when she left school."

Sara, after this somewhat lengthy explanation, was beginning to understand. "Jill has just arrived," she smiled. "I expect Katie was pleased to see her." Then, carefully, "I think I caught a glimpse of Katie while

I was looking for your house in Salen, but perhaps I was mistaken."

"No, you wouldn't be, at that." The little woman shook her neat grey head, a frown on her brown, sea-tanned face. "But I hope you'll not be thinking that she is taking time off behind your back. She peeped in for a minute to see me, and told me that she was taking a message from Miss Jill to a friend. She didn't say who the friend was, but as soon as she's been she is returning to the castle. That's what she said."

The sky above them darkened and suddenly heavy raindrops swept the windscreen. Sara groped swiftly for the wiper switch and flicked it on, clearing the windscreen instantly. "I hope she doesn't get wet," she smiled wryly, as the big car leapt forward.

"It's just a shower, I expect, and she doesn't mind the rain. We get quite a lot of it here." Obviously reassured by Sara's casual remark, Miss Black settled back in her seat again with a contented sigh.

Sara glanced at her quickly, her mind churning over the aspects of this new disclosure. It seemed a bit peculiar that Jill had sent Katie to Salen with a message, especially after saying that she was tired and couldn't be bothered with anything. And surely most of the people Jill knew would be easily available by telephone? It all seemed to point to some secret intrigue, but at the same time, Katie could have made up the story as an excuse to get away while Biddy was in bed. Sara frowned, impatient with herself for worrying.

Then suddenly a frightening thought struck her. That mysterious stranger with the beard had talked with a definite south country accent! It didn't bear thinking about, but could he possibly be the artist whom Jill was supposed to be in love with? But of course such a thought was quite ridiculous. He had got off the same boat as she had, almost three weeks ago. If he had been Jill's friend he would have waited until she had arrived before he came himself. She mustn't let her imagination and an over-developed sense of responsibility run away with her.

She drove slowly into the castle courtyard, and after helping Miss Black from the car took her up to see Biddy. After promising a cup of tea she left them talking.

As she was going through the door Biddy remembered to tell her that the doctor had called, and that he might come back in the morning.

"I don't rightly understand it," she complained impatiently to Sara. "Three times in as many days he is visiting me! I'm nearly scared to put my feet over the side of the bed, although my pains are almost gone!"

So Ian had come, Sara mused, as she ran downstairs. Hugh had been right. Or had he? She was no authority on the ways of a Highland doctor. Surely one or two visits to see a patient couldn't be construed as anything else but medical vigilance!

Jill, much to Sara's surprise, was in the kitchen. She swung around when she heard Sara, her face alight with anticipation which faded rapidly when she saw who it was. It would seem that she had expected someone else, and turned away with a frown as Sara, after a brief word of greeting, switched on the electric kettle to make the promised cup of tea.

"I'm just taking this up for Biddy," she explained, as Jill surveyed the tray she was preparing with raised eyebrows. "It's early yet. Katie will see to ours when she returns from Salen."

She phrased her sentence deliberately, and just as

deliberately watched for Jill's reactions as she spoke. There was a moment's silence, and although outwardly Jill gave no indication of alarm, Sara noticed a certain wariness creep into her eyes.

Then suddenly Jill laughed, turning away from Sara's sensitive face to sit in Biddy's empty chair by the fire. She leaned back and crossed her slim legs. Sara felt her watching her through half-closed lids and was vaguely irritated.

"Of course," Jill still smiled blandly, "you were going to Salen yourself, I remember, and you offered to take me. But I didn't know that Katie was going. You could have given her a lift."

Someone, for some reason or another, wasn't telling the truth. Carefully Sara opened the tea-caddy and measured three spoonfuls of tea-leaves into the warmed pot while she considered what Jill had said. If Jill was speaking the truth, then Katie wasn't. But why should Katie need to pretend that she was in Salen on an errand for Jill? Her time was usually her own between lunch and tea, and she didn't have to look for an excuse.

"Katie lives in Salen," she murmured, glancing again at Jill's smooth face. "I expect she just made up her mind to go and see her aunt. I brought Miss Black back with me to see Biddy. This is why I'm making early tea."

"Miss Black?" If Sara had hoped subconsciously to startle Jill, she succeeded. She sat up with a jerk, her childish face blank. "Not that old gossip?" she cried angrily. "That old woman talks so much—one can't believe the half of what she says!"

"Please...!" Sara threw up her hands defensively as she stared, startled, at the girl in the chair. Miss Black, she felt certain, was not a gossip, at least not in

94

the way Jill implied. But Jill was clearly upset that she had come here with her this afternoon. For the hundredth time Sara wondered why she had allowed Jane to persuade her to take this job. A typing job in a large impersonal city office would have been much better. At least it wouldn't have involved her intimately with a family like the Frasers who believed in riding roughshod over anyone who got in their way. Instead of weeks Sara felt that she had been here for years, so embroiled was she becoming in their affairs.

In self-defence she refused to worry any more about Katie and the stranger, or Jill for that matter, and was just about to add a sharp rejoinder to her initial exclamation when the telephone rang.

Jill, not usually quick to exert herself, jumped up with a surprising alacrity, and almost ran to answer it. With a resigned sigh Sara started to spread bread and butter.

Jill was back in a matter of minutes. "That was Beth Asquith," she said. Obviously having regained her composure, she sat down again in her chair with a satisfied grin. "She's mad because Hugh has gone and never told her. She wanted to know if he'll be back in time for the dance next Friday night."

"Dance?" Sara's eyebrows rose fractionally in spite of the traitorous surge of joy which rushed through her. She had thought they might have gone to London together.

"Oh, the *ceilidh*, you know." Jill's chattering tongue ran on. "Beth's mum gives a rather special one each June. Sometimes we come up specially for it. Not Hugh, of course. He's usually working overseas somewhere. I told Madam that I didn't think he would be here this year either, and she promptly rang off."

"But, Jill . . ." Sara stared frowning at Jill's mischievous face, "Hugh expects to be home in a day or two. He told me so himself."

"Did he now?" Jill replied, in silky undertones. "He isn't usually so precise about his movements."

"Don't be silly," Sara retorted coolly, but she felt her face grow hot at the hidden innuendo in Jill's remark. "I suppose you were only joking with Miss Asquith," she finished lamely.

"Don't talk rot." Jill grimaced inelegantly. "I don't like Miss Asquith any more than she likes me, so you needn't stand between us armed with diplomacy! I didn't see any reason to ressure her, and actually you never know with Hugh. He could be away for weeks if he felt like it."

"Are many *ceilidhs* held on the island?" Sara didn't want to contemplate the possibility of Hugh being away for weeks, and asked the question impulsively in an effort to regain her equilibrium.

"All through the winter," Jill told her briefly. "Mostly it's a case of people just dropping in for a chat and the odd song. Strong cups of tea and coffee, sandwiches and hot scones. If you like that sort of thing. Beth's mum gives a ball in aid of her favourite charity. Full regalia with all the trappings, but I don't know if I'll go this year. Hugh might take you if he does happen to be here."

Sara suddenly remembered Ian McKenzie's invitation. "Actually," she said impulsively, without really meaning to, "Dr McKenzie mentioned it yesterday morning."

"Oh, well . . ." Jill shrugged as if she couldn't care less, her small face completely indifferent. "It seems that you might be going one way or another. I'd hate Beth for a sister-in-law," she continued, almost in the same breath. "Although I suppose Hugh is bound to get married some time. Might make him a bit more human if he did," she muttered darkly, as Sara, fearing what she might hear next, departed hurriedly with the tea-tray.

Sara lingered deliberately with Biddy and her sister, unwilling to return to the kitchen to listen to more about Hugh and Beth Asquith, trying to convince herself that it was just because she disliked gossip. Wherever she looked there was Hugh, the moon glinting on his dark head as he bent over her.

Trying to rid herself of his image, she ran Miss Black home to Salen, getting back with barely enough time to prepare a simple dinner of soup and salad.

She was relieved to find that Jill was in her room. If Katie and she were scheming together then she didn't want to know about it, but Katie lulled her suspicions when she told her that she had been to see a friend who would come and cook until Biddy was properly better.

"If it's all right by you, miss," she smiled, "I know Jean will manage very nicely."

So much for that! Sara decided wryly next morning, as she ate breakfast once more in the dining room. Katie, happily, had gone on to say that Mr Fraser had suggested it before he went away. Sara hadn't known whether to be vexed or pleased. He might, she thought, have asked her opinion before overriding her in such a fashion! It would have saved her a lot of unnecessary worry if she had known exactly what Katie was doing in Salen. Once more his arrogance struck her forcibly.

However, she could not but admit that it was pleasant not to be responsible for the day's menu or the work involved in cooking all the meals. A sense of relaxation filled her, and she felt even better when the morning's mail brought a letter from Jane. Jane was busy at the office, but very soon she might take a short holiday. She had thought about coming to Mull. If Sara could let her know when it was convenient they might spend a few days together, even travel back together if Sara's work at Lochgoil happened to be finished.

Finished at Lochgoil? In spite of her pleasure in hearing from Jane, the bright morning sunshine seemed dimmer. Outside the air was sea-fresh with the faint scent of lilac drifting in through the open window. Apart from the distant sound of the waves breaking on the shore, all was silent. Around the inshore islands the seagulls would be crying incessantly, but in the house one couldn't hear them. Only a lark, its high vibrant notes rising clearly, gave any indication that another creature existed in the world besides herself. A sigh escaped her. Already she knew she would hate to leave it, for all her misgivings, yet here was Jane reminding her that the day would surely come when she must do just that.

For the rest of the morning Sara kept busy and saw little of Jill. She was just about to seek her out after lunch when Ian McKenzie arrived, ostensibly to see Biddy. He was there for about half an hour, the half of which he spent talking to Sara, trying again to persuade her to go with him to the dance, but as before, she found herself unable to give him a definite answer. She couldn't rid herself of the idea that Beth Asquith didn't like her, although their acquaintance had been short, and if this was so it seemed presumptuous to impose on her hospitality. With a regretful smile she saw Ian out and started to search for Jill.

When she couldn't find her she asked Katie who

was busy washing up their luncheon dishes, and had no idea.

"Maybe she's gone to see Miss Asquith," Katie suggested glibly. "She was telling me that the lady rang her only yesterday." As Sara stood frowning she turned up her radio loudly.

Sara refrained from retorting that she already had Jill's version of that phone call, and she thought it highly unlikely that Jill was there. And yet why not? People often professed to hate one another when in reality their dislike was only superficial. Even so, Sara wasn't convinced that she would find her with Beth. Of course Katie was only expressing an opinion. Jill could be anywhere.

There were no immediate neighbours, their nearest being some miles away down the coast. If it hadn't been for the telephone call Sara wouldn't have known where to start looking.

She had just decided to forget about Jill for the time being and spend an hour on the beach. It was still a beautiful day, and the sea and sunshine beckoned. For once there wasn't a great deal to do, and Biddy, in spite of her protests that she was better, was dozing comfortably in her bed. The big castle was quiet when the telephone shrilled rudely through the silence.

Sara, about to go out through the great front door, turned and ran quickly back up the twisting stairs to answer it, waving Katie back to her library book in the kitchen.

"Hello!" she cried breathlessly into the mouthpiece. To her surprise it was Beth Asquith.

"You sound anxious," Beth mocked coolly.

Sara clutched the receiver hard. "I'm sorry," she

murmured. "I was just leaving the castle. I thought it might be urgent."

"From London, perhaps?" Beth's voice drawled, full of purring, cat-like qualities, which slightly puzzled Sara until Beth added softly, "As a matter of fact I rang Hugh last night. When he's away he likes me to ring him up and talk to him. He'll be home in time for the dance, which was actually what I wanted to speak to you about. I saw Ian McKenzie in Salen after lunch and he said he would like to bring you along. I felt I must add a word of welcome myself."

Strangely uncharacteristic consideration! Beth didn't seem the sort to put herself out for a total stranger, especially one she hadn't seemed to like. But, Sara told herself uncertainly, she could be mistaken. One shouldn't really jump to such uncharitable conclusions after one short meeting.

"Thank you," she said quietly, while searching unhappily for an excuse. "You're very kind, but I'm not sure that I can get away. I should have to ask Mr Fraser. Besides, Biddy isn't well, and Jill has just arrived."

"What on earth has Jill to do with it?" Beth's shrill laughter stung Sara's ear. "I don't see why you need worry about her. She appears to be very cosy with a new boy-friend, an artist who's rented a cottage down the coast. I wonder if Hugh knows about it?"

"I'm sure you must be mistaken." With a start of dismay Sara protested hotly, refusing to believe what she instinctively knew to be the truth.

Beth laughed again, obviously enjoying the note of alarm she could hear in Sara's voice. "I can assure you that I am not! They appeared to be on the best of terms when I passed them a short while ago. But then the Frasers aren't renowned for wasting time—or hadn't you discovered?"

"Please!" In her agitation Sara dropped the receiver and stood staring at it as if it was red-hot. She ought to ring back and apologize. Beth would expect it. But she didn't know Beth's number and she didn't have the time or the inclination to look it up.

A peculiar sense of urgency overtook her. For a short while she had thought all her half-formed fears to be groundless, and now this! She must do something to help Jill. To warn her that Beth Asquith knew about her romance and would probably tell Hugh. From a jumble of reactions Sara found it impossible to be completely honest with herself. Was she doing this for Jill's sake, or because of a subconscious desire to please Hugh and keep her job here?

At all costs she must try to find Jill and judge for herself whether this artist was the unscrupulous bounder Hugh had told her about, or maybe another, quite acceptable friend. But how stupid she had been not to have kept her wits about her, and asked Beth the whereabouts of this man's cottage. She felt reluctant to approach Katie again, even though she now suspected that the girl could supply the information she was after.

With a frustrated sigh Sara dragged her eyes away from the telephone and picked up her coat. Then, out of the blue, she remembered Ian suggesting that she went with him down the coast to visit a patient. He had mentioned the ruined chapel of Pennygowan, where one of the early Macleans and his wife were said to have practised black magic. If Beth had seen both Ian and Jill since lunch, they must have been more or less in the same place. And she had seen Ian in Salen.

Sara drove the Jaguar swiftly away from the castle with renewed confidence. Jill, she knew, would be driving a small white Mini which her mother used when she visited Lochgoil, and which was kept in one of the outer garages. This was probably why she hadn't heard her go out earlier. Sara liked small cars herself, and didn't intend borrowing Hugh's Jaguar more than she could help, but she felt fully justified in taking it this afternoon.

In the village she stopped and asked a group of children if they knew of any holiday cottages in the district. While she didn't much like probing for information in this way, she felt it would be more discreet than asking in a shop or bar. The children would only conclude that she was some passing tourist seeking accommodation and forget about her as soon as she was out of sight.

To her dismay they told her that there were several cottages in the area but that most of them would be let at this time of the year.

She was just about to thank them and drive off when one small girl piped up.

"Mr Matheson down the road has two. One's let to an artist man, but my dad says the other one's empty because the roof rains in. If you wouldn't be fussy maybe Mr Matheson would let you have that . . ."

It was surprising how easily she found the cottage after all. Situated near the Forsa river, at the end of a long rutted lane, it looked so old it almost blended into the brown landscape, and apart from a thin trickle of smoke from one stumpy chimney there was no visible sign of life.

Sara approached cautiously. She had left the Jaguar just off the main road, too fearful of its springs to bring it down a track such as this. She hadn't rehearsed or even thought what she was going to say, and as she knocked carefully on the worn front door she prayed fervently that she would find the right words.

After a few short seconds, which seemed like hours, the young man with the beard flung open the door. If Sara had expected him to look put out she was disappointed, but he did look surprised.

"Well, well," he drawled, "if it isn't the girl off the boat. Mr Fraser's secretary, I presume?" A mocking smile on his face, he leant against the collapsible door-post, his hands thrust negligently into his trouser pockets. Sara drew back a fraction, startled. This was certainly the same young man whom she had seen repeatedly, but whether he was the one Hugh was worried about she had yet to find out. She flushed, biting her bottom lip nervously as he regarded her with derisive eyes.

But before she could speak there was a slight movement behind him and Jill appeared. Her small vivid face was disdainful as her eyes slipped over Sara. She was obviously far from pleased to see who it was.

"You're mistaken, Colin." She laughed without mirth. "Private detective Winton would be more appropriate!"

Sara stared; she felt shattered, bereft of words, but as their eyes met she could see that the other girl had been hurt, and that she was very much on the defensive. She felt an outsider suddenly, as though she were standing outside a circle which she had deliberately split.

Somehow she must get through to Jill and her friend that she was here to help them, rather than because she worked for Hugh. Instinctively she knew that this man was indeed the artist from London. It had been fairly obvious from the moment he had opened the door.

"I'm sorry, Jill," she said quietly, her eyes still on her scornful face. "I know it looks suspicious, but I didn't come to pry. I came to help, to warn you, if you like. Someone knows about Colin being here, and it's probably only a matter of time before Hugh finds out."

"Beth Asquith. I knew it!" Jill's face went red with temper. "That awful bitch!"

"Jill!" Sara remonstrated, keeping her own temper under control with an effort. "You know as well as I do that such abuse won't get you anywhere. It certainly wouldn't help your case with your brother. Suppose we go inside and talk this over in a rational manner?"

For a moment she thought Jill was going to refuse, that only Colin's weight against the door prevented Jill from slamming it in her face, then with a shrug the girl turned and Colin stepped back to give Sara room to follow her inside.

The living room, Sara noticed, was clean but untidy. An easel stood in one corner surrounded by artist's paraphernalia of canvases, tubes of paint and brushes, while a pile of cameras and photographic equipment covered a small dining table by the window. A peat fire smouldering in the hearth took the chill off the air and managed to convey a degree of comfort.

Sara sat down cautiously on a rather rickety wooden chair which Colin silently pulled out from beneath the table. The two armchairs looked cosy but could scarcely be seen under a pile of suitcases and clothing. He still hadn't added anything to his first remark in the doorway.

Jill, perched on top of a stool, glanced from him back to Sara sullenly. "I'm sorry, Sara," she said abruptly but in slightly warmer tones. "I suppose to you this all looks like a string of lies and intrigue, but Colin and I really are in love and want to get married. Sometimes one is driven to say the wrong things out of sheer self-defence. You probably don't know, but neither Hugh or Mummy would even bother to meet Colin. They condemned him out of hand because he's an artist. They seem to imagine he's starving in a garret!"

Sara frowned, her blue eyes thoughtful. She remembered Hugh admitting that he hadn't met Jill's boy-friend. Surely no one had the right to dismiss the feelings of others so sweepingly. And maybe Mrs Fraser, only recently bereaved and with business worries in America, had forgotten how painful such criticism and indifference could be.

Mentally Sara strove to weigh things up. While feeling sorry for Jill she must be careful. The little minx could be very appealing, but was probably capable of deceiving anyone if she put her mind to it.

She sighed wryly, looking rather unhappily at Jill again. "Surely you could have contrived a meeting of some sort, Jill? I wouldn't have thought you lacking in ingenuity."

Jill shot Colin a quick glance as she shook her head. "I'm afraid someone told Mum a weird story about Colin. It wasn't true and I tried to convince her, but she refused to believe me, and you know how things blow up. After that I did everything I could to keep them apart. I suppose that actually Hugh got her version when he came home. Anyway, he read me a lecture and things have been a bit precarious ever since."

It took little effort to imagine that lecture along with Hugh's uncomprising attitude. Sara could guess its devastating effect.

"Suppose," she said slowly to Jill, while looking rather pointedly towards Colin, "you start afresh by introducing me to your friend? Then we can consider one or two possibilities."

CHAPTER SIX

THE occasional drone of a bee drifted in on the warm fresh air through the open window. The sound was relaxing and slightly soporific and made Sara realize that she was tired. But the atmosphere in the small cottage room was too tense to allow for relaxation.

Jill alarmed Sara by sitting quite still, a deep frown on her defiant face, almost as if she disliked her proposal. There was a long awkward silence. Then suddenly, with a careless shrug she slid off the stool and going over to Colin, drew him forward.

"I suppose," she stared broodingly at Sara, "I've been behaving rather childishly, but I just didn't think. Anyway, as you insist, this is Colin Brown, arch-villain from London!"

Colin glanced from Jill to Sara with a quirk of amusement as he held out his hand. For the first time Sara really saw him properly. He was tall, and in the dim light his young face seemed all bone and hollow, and his mouth curiously strained in spite of his casual demeanour.

"So we meet properly at last, Miss Winton." His dark eyebrows rose as he looked at her closely. "I must confess to having seen you since the day I rescued your bag, but I thought it wiser to keep my distance. I might have known you would catch up with me sooner or later." He grinned as he pulled Jill to him affectionately. "Now I can see you're wondering just what Jill and I are cooking up between us."

"Well, that's putting it rather bluntly, Mr Brown." Sara met his twinkling grey eyes and returned his smile. She liked his firm handshake. "I'll admit," she went on, "to being slightly worried. Would you think me over-curious if I asked what you do exactly? There are so many different kinds of artists."

"Not at all." His voice was quietly confident as he glanced at Jill. "I started with a big firm as a commercial artist. Then I went freelance. It was a bit hazardous to begin with, but now I'm doing quite well. I work chiefly as an illustrator and enjoy doing the odd landscape. At the moment I'm doing birds and animals for a new children's book with a Highland setting."

"But you came up three weeks ago?"

Colin smiled wryly, hugging Jill's arm. "To get some work done before Jill arrived. It seemed rather callous leaving her in hospital, but actually she insisted. You see, I like to photograph my subject before I paint it. It helps as a check for colour and detail, and when Jill's with me she talks so much that she scares every bird within miles."

"And how," Sara looked patiently at both of them, "did you expect to remain here undetected? Hugh is bound to find out."

"It was a chance," Jill declared mutinously, "and we took it. Hugh only intended being here for a short time to wrap up the estate. Now he talks of living here permanently, so I suppose he's bound to find out one of these days."

Sara's heart gave a sudden lurch. If, as Jill said, Hugh intended staying here, perhaps he would keep her on as his secretary, if he needed one. And if this was wise! She knew a crazy urge to be in his arms again, to feel his lips on hers, moving with unspoken desire against her own.

She drew a quick trembling breath, thrusting his image to one side. "I really think, Jill, you should take Colin to see him and state your case clearly. After all, Hugh couldn't stop you from marrying, as you're over eighteen."

"But I like my family," Jill protested, a little too vehemently, before Colin could speak. "I would rather have their approval."

"Look," Sara glanced swiftly at her watch, "I must get back or they'll be sending out a search party. It's almost five. I suggest you follow me, Jill, and we'll try to come to some decision later this evening. After dinner, perhaps."

"The sooner the better," Colin agreed tersely, as he followed them out of the cottage. "This hole and corner business doesn't appeal to me."

Despite various interruptions dinner went off smoothly, but before Sara could pin Jill down to a constructive course of action Beth called with two young friends.

Thinking about Jill's love affair, as she helped Katie prepare an extra pot of coffee, it seemed to Sara that there was nothing that a little common sense couldn't put right. Colin Brown, at close quarters, appeared to be a very likeable young man and, if what he said was true, with a very promising future. If Jill would let her broach the subject to Hugh when he returned, Sara felt sure she could make him take a more realistic view of things. Not that she looked forward to such an interview, but it seemed quite clear that someone must try to straighten out a situation which had apparently only arisen from a series of misunderstandings in the first place. It would be much better, she felt, if Jill was allowed to see Colin without further opposition. It would at least enable her to see her romance in its proper perspective without this unnatural aura of drama.

For the next hour Sara poured coffee, passed biscuits, and made herself generally useful in the background. If Beth Asquith remembered their sharp exchange earlier on the telephone, she made no reference to it, indeed, contrarily, she seemed to go out of her way to be charming, even to the extent of renewing her invitation to the dance in such a way that Sara found it impossible to refuse. But it was Jill's attitude which puzzled her most. Why, she wondered, was the girl gushing so now over Beth? Again a definite feeling of mistrust smote Sara. In the end she gave up trying to fathom it out, and after washing up the empty coffee cups and seeing Biddy comfortably settled for the night, she went to bed herself with an aching head.

Jill sought her out next morning in the library as she was filing away the morning's mail. It was almost midday, but Jill still yawned sleepily, as if she had been up half the night. "I'm awfully sorry, darling, but I'm tired," she explained unnecessarily. "Beth was late in going and when I looked in you were fast asleep. I almost woke you up, but you seemed to be having such pleasant dreams. Who were you dreaming about—Ian McKenzie?"

"Jill!" Sara turned rather impatiently to look at her, brushing back her long fair hair which she had been too busy to tie back before breakfast. "I had a busy day yesterday trying to sort out your affairs, and this morning I slept in. Now just tell me what it is that you want, then leave me to get finished here."

She wasn't sure that she should be talking to her employer's sister in this fashion, but with Jill she had discovered it was little use beating about the bush.

However, Jill wasn't so easily discouraged. "Please, Sara," she begged, "don't be cross. I must have a word with you, in case Hugh comes home unexpectedly. It would just be like him!"

Attractively dressed in wide blue trousers, she perched neatly on the edge of Sara's desk, staring at her with huge appealing eyes. "It's about Colin. I don't want Hugh to know that he's here. At least not straight away. Let it stew for a while—until Mum returns, perhaps?"

"But, Jill," Sara exclaimed, "don't you think if you won Hugh around you'd have crossed your biggest hurdle? And," she added deliberately, "how about Miss Asquith? She knows about Colin, even if she doesn't know the details."

"I know!" Jill shrugged indifferently. "But somehow I don't think she'll spill the beans. If she wants me for a sister-in-law she knows she has to treat me right."

Jill didn't like opposition. Her bottom lip stuck out peevishly.

"Would Miss Asquith let a small thing like that deter her?" Sara queried drily, stung by Jill's egotistical reasoning.

"You'd be surprised," Jill smirked shrewdly. "I may be Hugh's stepsister, but his father is just like a father to me, and Hugh's awfully fond of Mum. And I certainly could tell him a thing or two about his darling Beth!"

"Jill—Jill, be quiet!" Defensively Sara placed her palms flat over her ears and turned away from the girl's determined little face. Why did she feel either years older or younger than Jill, never the same age? She took a breath and tried to attack from another direction. "I wonder if you quite realize what you're asking. I'm to turn a blind eye while you spend hours in a lonely cottage with a stranger? Here on the island where you're so well known, in fact anywhere, it just wouldn't be ethical. Besides, I think Colin would agree."

"Of course he would," Jill retorted with smug sarcasm. "He's almost as strait-laced as you are. And if that's all that's worrying you I'm able to set your mind at rest. He rang this morning to say that his sister has arrived for a fortnight, so we should be well chaperoned."

Sara stared at Jill for a full minute before she spoke. There was too much to assimilate in too short a time, and she had a sinking feeling that it would take a brain much brighter than hers to weigh the situation up properly. However, there seemed no harm in allowing Jill and Colin this chance to get their relationship sorted out properly. Without opposition and its attendant stimulation, they might even discover they weren't really so much in love after all.

She looked at Jill squarely as she jumped to her feet. "All right, then," she said stiffly. "If what you say is true, then I won't say anything to Hugh, but neither will I deliberately cover up for you. You refuse to tell him yourself, and if he finds out some other way, well—just don't expect my sympathy!"

Before Sara had time to fully realize the enormity of her promise to Jill, Hugh came home. He came that same day, in the evening after dinner, walking in while she was sitting talking to Beth, who had called again unexpectedly on some slight pretext which Sara felt she was in no position to question. Jill, who had been out all afternoon, was obviously tired, and yawned fitfully as she turned over the pages of a month-old magazine.

Beth saw him first as he opened the door.

"Good heavens!" she exclaimed, a proprietorial air touching her delighted smile. "We didn't expect you so soon. Have you had dinner?"

"Yes," he said, briefly returning Beth's smile, and Sara twisted her head to look at him as he removed his heavy leather jacket before crossing to the fire. Underneath the jacket he wore one of his thick white sweaters which as usual seemed to emphasize his height and breadth of shoulder. His glance went from Beth to Sara, who for one taut moment saw herself reflected in the darkness of his eyes before he turned to Beth again. "I flew up with Jim Dixon from Carsaig. He conveniently happened to be in London on business."

"But you're sure you've had dinner?" Beth asked again. Almost as if she was already mistress of the house, Sara decided, as Hugh with an audible sigh of relief sat down.

"I had it at Carsaig. Jenny would have me stay. Jim ran me home, but he's had a long day and wouldn't come in. A cup of coffee would be welcome, though, if you have one handy?"

"We've just finished." Beth smiled, her eyes sparkling smugly. "Sara—or Jill, perhaps you could ring."

But Sara was already on her feet, clutching the cold coffee tray as if it was a lifebelt. Anything to escape Hugh's darkly devastating eyes! "I'll make some fresh," she said swiftly. "It's Katie's evening off. She and Jean have gone down to the village."

Bewilderingly he was by her side in a trice, ignoring Beth's frown, taking the tray from her. "Let me," he grinned smoothly. "I'll come and get it. There are one or two things I'd like to discuss."

Sara paused, then Jill astonished her by jumping up and suggesting over-brightly, "Why not let me—rather than fight about it, Hugh?" She reached up and kissed him lightly on one cheek. "It's nice to have you back, and if I get the perishing coffee you can sit back and relax. Your business with Sara can't be that urgent!"

To Sara's surprise he didn't argue. He thrust the tray passively into Jill's outstretched hands, and promptly did as he was told.

Sara watched as he stretched his long legs and gave his attention to Beth again.

"You must be extremely tired, Hugh darling," Beth remarked, her thin voice oozing sympathy as she regarded him tenderly. "But if you want to speak to Miss Winton about something, don't mind me. Go right ahead." Her sharp eyes glanced at Sara derisively.

Sara bit her lip, unconsciously resentful. It seemed that he enjoyed making her a target for Beth's disparaging remarks. She stared at him with a kind of helpless, unexplainable anger, until he turned his head. The dark eyes mocked and his shapely mouth twisted sardonically as he guessed what was on her mind. It was an effort to look away, and his next words enveloped her like a cloud.

"What I have to say to Miss Winton will keep for five minutes. We can go to the library later."

Behind his words lay just the trace of a threat. What was she guilty of now? She shivered, wondering why this enigmatical man should arouse such a complex of feelings.

"Any time you wish," she agreed readily enough. forcing a smile to her lips, reluctant to reveal even a hint of unrest, especially before Beth. But her voice sounded breathless even to herself as a hundred doubts nervously invaded her head.

He was home sooner than anyone expected. Although Sara definitely remembered him saying that he would be back in a day or two, she hadn't taken it literally. Had some new business cropped up in connection with Lochgoil? Something, perhaps, which could only be sorted out from this end? Or could it be Jill? Had some hidden aspect of her romance come to light? In London maybe he had discovered the whereabouts of Colin Brown!

Such thoughts could only be painfully confusing. Sara ruthlessly clamped down, listening silently as Hugh talked to Beth about friends and acquaintances in London. She received the impression of time well spent, but not of any great catastrophe! It was a relief when Jill came back at last with fresh hot coffee.

"Any news of Mum, Hugh?" Jill asked, smiling, as she sat down beside him and poured it out.

Hugh shot her a lazy glance, slightly watchful. "I was in touch from London," he told her. "She could be home very soon, probably within the next two weeks."

Sara noticed that Jill's cheeks went pink. "She might have rung me," she retorted indignantly. "I've scarcely heard from her since she left. Why should she phone you?"

"It was mostly business, my dear," he said placatingly, drinking his coffee off in one long draught and refilling his cup himself. "And actually I rang her."

"You'll be hearing very soon, Jill, I'm sure," Beth frowned at Jill with a slightly reproving smile which made her seem much older. "You know she has a lot on her mind."

"On holiday!" Jill snorted, staring sullenly at Beth.

"You're tired, Jill." Hugh put down his cup with sharp emphasis. "And it's getting late." He stared pointedly at the clock. "Beth was just saying she must be going, and I would like a word with Sara before she goes to bed. If you would go along to the library, Sara, I'll join you in a minute, after I've seen Beth off." His eyes slewed to where Sara sat very upright in her chair.

Sara looked away from him quickly as she rose to her feet, pausing just long enough to say tensely, "If you don't mind I'll pop and see Biddy first. I'll be as quick as I can."

Not daring to keep him waiting, she flew upstairs to make sure that Biddy was comfortable for the night. She had taken her some hot milk and biscuits about nine o'clock, and now she found her just dozing off. It seemed to please her greatly to know that Hugh was home again.

"I'm very thankful that Mr Hugh's back safely," she cried. "Indeed I have never cared for those flying machines!"

She smiled happily as Sara tucked her in gently and switched off the light.

"How is she?" Hugh asked, as Sara entered the library and closed the door. He was standing in front of the fireplace with his hands behind his back, and she felt curiously at a disadvantage as she took a few hesitant steps into the middle of the room.

"Much better," she said simply as he waited. "The rest in bed is helping her a lot."

He considered this briefly. "Did the good doctor produce a magic pill, or have you succeeded where others have failed? I've never known Biddy to stay in bed before."

"Perhaps a combination of both," Sara murmured

116

demurely. Somehow she was reluctant to tell him that Ian had been here three days running, which might have convinced Biddy that she was worse than she actually was, with the desired effect! "Apart from her rheumatism I really think she needs a rest. Apparently she hasn't had a holiday in years, and this is a very big place to run."

"Yes, of course." Hugh spoke testily, seeming to lose interest, his mind on other things.

Sara stirred, ill at ease. The night breeze drifting in through the open window brought with it a myriad scents and the distant sound of the sea. Suddenly she felt weary, in a trance of tiredness and over-emotionalism. Waiting for him to speak, she stared at him closely, until it seemed that every feature of his face was impressed on her memory. Helplessly she averted her eyes.

"You didn't bring me here to talk about Biddy," she prompted.

"I didn't," he returned hardily. "But you don't look in any particular condition to carry on any sort of discussion. What have you been doing with yourself while I've been away?"

For a second Sara hesitated, her eyes widening. She wasn't aware that the overhead light shone directly on her face, enhancing every angle. She had chosen to wear a thin black jersey dress with a low rounded neckline which emphasized the whiteness of her skin and the fragility of her slender bones. Her hair was loose, falling across her shoulders in a cloud of spun silk from a centre parting.

Her voice came guarded. "I've been busy, I'll admit, but nothing to make a fuss about."

"I see." He walked over to where she still stood in the middle of the room and drew her over to the fire.

His fingers caught around her waist, curiously without tenderness.

"Let me see just how busy you've been." As they stood there he tilted her chin, his fingers retaining that same degree of hardness, while his eyes examined the faint shadows on her pale cheeks.

"Please," she protested, agitation quickening her voice, yet unable to move.

A faint sensual hostility stirred in his face. Abruptly he shook his head. "You're very lovely—and tempting," he murmured, frowning.

Sara hadn't imagined that hostility. She wrenched away from him.

"You might think me beautiful, but you don't like me, do you?"

His eyes went black. "I don't like the things a woman can do to a man, if that's what you mean."

"That's something quite different."

"How women love to complicate the issue," he said briefly. "Born to make trouble."

"You can't load us all into the one basket." Sara tilted her head at him. "Some women have made men very happy."

"No," he disagreed suavely. "It's usually the other way around. Always it's the male who must make the effort. So far as you're concerned, I don't think I do like you, but as I said once before, I shall have to put up with you until we're finished here."

He stood only inches away from her, his eyes travelling critically down the fragile bones of her throat and shoulders. "Such vulnerability ... I suppose the death of your parents did that to you."

Sara stood rooted to the spot, shaken, shocked, incapable of thought. How had he found out? Why was he doing this to her? Her hands moved convulsively, warding him off, trying to convey a revulsion she couldn't find words to express.

"How did you find out?" she whispered at last. "How could you have known?" Her throat went tight. like a newly re-opened wound she felt the pain spreading.

He held her now, his grip on her upper arms almost as hurtful as the pain in her heart, forcing her head back so that she must look into his eyes. Was he entirely without mercy!

His dark eyes held hers. "You said to Ian Mc-Kenzie—my father was a doctor. Was! Spelt out in capital letters. Ian probably didn't notice, but it aroused my curiosity."

"So you poked around?" Distraught, Sara's voice rose bitterly.

"Exactly." He regarded the rawness of her feelings unemotionally.

Sara could have hit him. Not for the first time, either! The primitive strength of her anger was barely controllable. "How?" she choked furiously through clenched teeth.

"I saw your friend Jane this morning before I left. I had an appointment with James Kerr."

"Which couldn't concern me."

"I intended to find out." He added with smooth purpose, "Jane was there and I took the opportunity."

The air between them was static, charged by electricity and anger that burnt.

She said, "You thought Daddy had been struck off? That he'd done something disreputable!"

He made a sound of complete exasperation. "I didn't give a damn. I just wanted to know what made you tick, that's all. What lies behind that intriguing element of sensitivity. I thought perhaps a man, an unhappy love affair. Since you came you've impressed yourself quite indelibly on my imagination."

Her face grew remote with an encroaching coldness. "And now that you've done your research and the mystery is cleared up I'm no longer of interest."

He gave a brief laugh, his eyes totally watchful on her distrait face, narrowed slightly. "I wouldn't say that, but first we must get rid of this inner torment." He shook her softly, his fingers gripping firmly the smooth skin of her arms. "You'll get over it, you know. It's a traumatic experience, but first you must strip down to rock bottom and start again. Until you face your loss squarely you couldn't hope for any sort of tranquillity."

Sara fought back burning hot tears. "Your philosophy astounds me, also your hardness!"

His smile was cynical but not unkind as he regarded her flushed cheeks. "Life goes on, Sara. If you want to go with it you learn to live with your sorrows, not let them take over."

"You call grieving for lost parents unnatural?"

"The way you're doing it, yes. As soon as I had a good look at you I knew. It stood out a mile. Something was eating you up. It showed in a thousand different ways."

And she had thought that no one could ever guess. Cups of bitterness invariably overflowed! "I hate you for asking Jane!" Indiscriminately Sara attacked again, yet feeling totally defenceless against his harsh logic. Her eyes continued to shimmer, but no tears fell. "I told her I felt better. Now she'll be worried."

"She was quite happy when I left," Hugh murmured ambiguously. "We talked."

"I see . . ." For a moment she was nonplussed. Her eyes widened. This she had not expected. Dared she ask what they had talked about? She could almost guess. Jane would do most of the talking, prompted by the odd glib question. Now this hard implacable man would possess her history, right up to date from the cradle, because to Jane she was the daughter she had never had, and never could have now, even if she married again.

Sara stirred like a sleepwalker, her blue eyes dilated, reflecting an unconscious plea for consolation.

He ground out, "What you need now is an emotional upheaval of a different kind. Something too big for you to cope with. Something which would sweep away those last remnants of self-pity you so tenaciously hold on to."

"Such as?" Sara's voice was no louder than a whisper, but the inflection spoke of an inner resistance. This man was used to pushing people around, probably to the limit of their physical and mental endurance, in order to attain his ends. Anything which hindered peak productivity must be removed. A secretary must be nothing more than a robot, her mind void of any emotion that might interfere with her job. By what method this was achieved he obviously didn't care.

He stared down at her darkly. "An emotional upheaval can usually be described as a love affair. Perhaps you should concentrate on Ian McKenzie. I don't think he would be reluctant, not where you're concerned. There are times when I find you quite enchanting myself."

Of its own accord Sara's hand shot out, but before it could reach his taunting face he caught it in his hard grip, bringing it down in front of him, hurting her as she had intended hurting him.

"I don't understand you!" she gasped, half sobbing,

her body sagging weakly as he jerked her to him.

His hand half-mooned her chin, his fingers steely as they slid behind her ear, grasping and twisting a handful of hair so that her head came back to his shoulder. She could feel in him no tenderness but a leashed anger.

His arms exploded a locked well of reserve. Sara's mouth suddenly yearned for his kisses, a strange hunger which raced through her body, not easily denied by the wavering strength of her mind.

But the strain of the last hour was telling on her. She looked white and exhausted, and as Hugh became aware of this his expression changed subtly and his arms slackened. With a half-smothered exclamation he thrust her quickly away from him into the depth of a large armchair, while he poured her a brandy, standing over her until she drank it down.

A slight smile smoothed the deep furrow on his brow. "At least you can cope with that," he said grimly. "It would have been more in character if you'd choked and spluttered."

"I'm not quite so juvenile as you think." She swallowed the drink, not because she particularly wanted it, but as an essential means of regaining the composure she had lost a few minutes ago. After a slight pause she felt able to say calmly, "Daddy's one weakness, perhaps, was a brandy with his coffee, and sometimes Mummy and I would join him."

"Nice for father," Hugh added sardonically. "And now, my child, if you don't mind pushing off, I have work to do."

"But you said—" Startled, Sara put down her empty glass with a small clatter. She took a deep breath. "You said there were things to discuss. Business?"

His smile was ironic as he towered over her. "That was before I got sidetracked, and I intend getting rid of you before it happens again. You've a little colour back in your cheeks, but I don't want you passing out on me any more tonight. Tomorrow we can discuss business to our hearts' content."

He held out an impersonal hand which she chose to ignore as she rose rather unsteadily to her feet. Her limbs still trembled slightly and she blamed the brandy while knowing that the real cause lay in the still uneven beating of her heart.

But it didn't help when he turned away abruptly and reached for a cigarette. In the blue flame from his lighter he inhaled deeply before asking offhandedly,

"Is Jill quite fit now, do you think?"

Sara stumbled, startled, on her way to the door. She had just been about to bid him goodnight when his query descended on her hapless head. She didn't turn as she murmured 'yes', unwilling that he should see her face. For the life of her she couldn't add anything more.

"Well, don't look as though you'd been shot in the back," he said impatiently. "As a matter of fact I thought I might take her to Iona tomorrow. I can mix it in with a bit of business, so it won't be time wasted. Have you ever been there yourself? Would you like to come?"

Nervously she half turned towards him, her profile taut under the light. Jill, she felt certain, wouldn't want to go. Not without Colin. But Hugh didn't know that Colin was here and she'd promised not to tell.

What a mix-up! Why in heaven's name had she agreed to keep the girl's secret? Why hadn't she had the sense to realize just what it would involve?

"Suppose," she suggested desperately, still not looking at him but sensing that he waited, "we leave it until the morning? You know what Jill is. She could have made other arrangements. After all, you didn't say when you were coming home."

And that, she decided as she took a quick shower next morning, had been the best she could do. Hurriedly she dressed. She hoped to find Jill and to warn her of Hugh's intentions before he found her himself. If Jill didn't want to go to Iona then she would have to wriggle out of the trip as best she could. Jill, Sara resolved, must make her own excuses. It would be bad enough if Hugh found out her own complicity without adding further to her list of crimes.

She would love to visit Iona, to see the famous cathedral and the burial ground of so many Scottish kings. Numerous tourists from all over the world went every year, but once her work here was finished Sara knew she would never return. This might be the only chance she would ever get to see the island.

Her head ached suddenly. She opened her handbag, searched inside, and brought out a bottle of aspirin, taking two, drinking from a glass of water. She wanted to go to Iona, but not alone with Hugh. Not right away, after last night. There hadn't been enough time to marshal her thoughts or get her emotions under complete control. Not yet could she face the intimacy of an afternoon spent together, but if Jill refused to go perhaps Hugh would change his mind and decide to go another day.

Jill wasn't in her room, and to Sara's surprise when she went in to breakfast Jill was almost finished. She had been out riding with Hugh, she said, and had agreed to go to Iona.

Sara stopped with her cup half-way to her lips. She said, sharply despairing, "Just like that! And to think I've hardly been able to sleep!"

"Why not?" Jill's babyish lips parted innocently. "As a matter of fact, darling Sara, Colin's sister is not my cup of tea. All she wants to do all day is hike around the moors. She's as mad about this bird-watching business as Colin, but for different reasons."

"Such as . . . ?"

"Well, you know Colin has to do it to get all the photographs he needs as a check for his work. Now he's got all he needs and could easily finish off his paintings in London, but Gwen demands an escort! I suspect he's been secretly bitten by the bug."

"What bug?" Jill talked in riddles, and used jargon so freely that sometimes it was difficult to keep up.

"Bird-watching!" Jill retorted irritably. "You're not very bright this morning, are you? Well, without asking me he actually told Gwen that he wouldn't mind going with her. Well, I've certainly told him that I mind!" Her small face fell sullenly. "But you don't know Colin."

"How could I?" Sara replied cautiously. "We've only met once. I thought you were in love with him?"

"I am—I am!" Jill's fists beat a tattoo upon the table. "But I'm not blind to his faults. He argues too much and he's too stubborn! He has the same crazy idea as you about telling Hugh. It took me ages yesterday to persuade him otherwise, and now he says that if we want a chaperon we've got to humour her!"

Good for Colin! Sara silently applauded as she hid a smile. Jill might not find her particular brand of humour amusing. But the more Sara learnt about Colin the better she felt she liked him. With him Jill would not get all her own way. Jill had been spoilt, and if Colin refused to carry on with the spoiling, then good for him. A little opposition wouldn't do her any harm!

"So . . . ?" she prompted, buttering a fresh piece of toast.

"So I've told Hugh that I'll be delighted to go to Iona after lunch." Jill's eyebrows rose with airy indifference. "It's all wrapped up. Katie is to look after Biddy. Colin will look after his sister, while you and I will be looked after by darling Hugh." She leant back in her chair, stretching her arms behind her head before lighting a cigarette and remarking lightly, "I might even find out what my dear old mum's up to in America, if I play my cards right."

"Jill!" Really, the girl was incorrigible. Sara's sigh carefully tempered a thrill of delight. It would be wonderful to visit Iona, but not if Jill was to pester Hugh all the time. His patience was finely balanced. If Jill probed, however ingeniously, he would be quickly aware of this and annoyed.

Sara, only too conscious of his black moods and his sharply destructive tongue, felt driven to intervene.

"Please, Jill," she pleaded quietly, "why not forget about your problems, just for one afternoon?"

"O.K.," Jill grinned repentantly as she jumped to her feet. "I'm truly sorry, Sara, and I promise to behave, if you'll just hold the fort while I go and see Colin. He must understand that this morning he belongs to me. Gwen can have him for the remainder of the day, if she wants him."

CHAPTER SEVEN

THE weather was beautiful as they started out. They got away before one o'clock after an early lunch. Hugh drove the Land-Rover, with Sara and Jill sitting in the front beside him. There was still, as on that first journey, a conglomeration of things in the back, but today Sara didn't seem to notice. Already, after a few short weeks on the island, she was losing a little of her delicate fastidiousness.

To her surprise Hugh too remembered that first day and teased her about it. "You looked quite put out," he grinned wickedly.

"Small wonder!" Jill wryly flew to her defence. "This old truck's always loaded with junk and oily smells. Not a place for the finicky!" She wrinkled her small nose.

Sara laughed. It was refreshing to find Jill in a good humour. "I expect the old junk comes in useful," she remarked happily.

All the way down the deeply indented west coast Jill chatted breezily about London, while Sara sat back, content to gaze at the passing landscape which she realized that the others must have seen many times before.

She was secretly amused to find that Hugh could more than cope with his sister's sometimes crafty remarks, interspersing them with slightly more logical views of his own. But she was also discovering that in spite of her rather childish ways Jill could be very intelligent when she felt like it, and she wondered if the girl had ever thought of a career. It might have channelled all that nervous restlessness into more rewarding spheres. A light sigh escaped her. Probably, like herself, Jill had been over-protected, as Hugh had so ruthlessly pointed out last night. It was perhaps a pity that he didn't apply the same theory to Jill, although she doubted whether he would recommend the same remedy for both of them.

After a night of rain the skies had cleared from the west to give an almost cloudless sky. As the sun struck hot against the inside of the Land-Rover Sara struggled out of her anorak, which was becoming uncomfortably warm. Underneath, her thin denim trousers and shirt felt cooler, and with a ribbon from her pocket she tied back her heavy hair from her face.

"You'd better not forget your anorak when you get out," Hugh warned, glancing at her quickly as she moved awkwardly in the confined space. "You might need it later."

"I won't," she murmured, looking away from him as she turned to drop the jacket behind her. Seated tightly in the middle between him and Jill, she could feel the hard pressure of his leg when she moved and her heart shook.

Defensively she edged nearer to Jill, feeling Hugh's mocking eyes resting on her hot face. She tried to keep her own eyes steadily on the road ahead, tracing her pale, nervous hands over her temples, hoping desperately that the clarity of her thoughts didn't show.

She felt a sense of relief when they passed through the village of Gribun and he told her briefly about a huge boulder set between two houses on the roadside.

Apparently in the last century a young couple had come to live there on their wedding night. But a violent storm had blown up, and a huge rock had crashed from the cliffs above, crushing the house and occupants, who were never seen again.

Sara shuddered as Hugh paused reflectively, but Jill only shrugged and said lightly, "Hugh's off on his hobbyhorse again, Sara. For goodness' sake don't encourage him, or we will never reach Iona today!"

He replied drily over Sara's head as his foot touched the accelerator, "One day, Jill, you might feel a certain sympathy."

"But not an obsession with the past!"

Sara's sensitive ears caught Hugh's impatient sigh as he drove swiftly on. "Time isn't relevant. It would be a tragedy in any age."

Jill sniffed. "But you did say that given time one can get over most things?"

"Exactly. But I didn't imply that one forgets completely."

Listening to their polite sparring, Sara became convinced that in some way it related to a previous conversation regarding Colin, and her body tensed with apprehension. With Jill there was no knowing what she would come out with next, and even though she had promised to behave, that was no guarantee that she would. Being so much in love it must be difficult for Jill always to hide her resentment, but after all, it was partly her own fault that she had chosen to hide Colin instead of making another attempt to sort things out.

As they argued it seemed to Sara that there existed between the two of them a light camaraderie, but little genuine understanding, and she was relieved when Hugh, as if tiring of the topic, suddenly started talking about something else.

The southern half of Mull appealed to her. It was

very mountainous and rugged, but Jill only looked bored when she pointed this out, and didn't reply.

"One day we'll come down and explore some of this area properly," Hugh smiled, apparently pleased at Sara's interest. But she wondered if, like his bird-watching promise, he would ever remember.

Jill wanted to stop at Bunessan farther along the coast and grumbled when Hugh insisted that there wasn't time. "I promised to meet John Finley at two o'clock," he explained. "I don't want to keep him waiting."

Jill stared at her brother crossly. "You didn't ask Beth today," she retaliated, with the obvious intention of annoying him, Sara thought curiously.

"A bit late in mentioning it," Hugh retorted drily. "As it happens she's very busy with preparations for the ball, but she's coming to dinner this evening."

He must have asked Beth to dinner when he had seen her out last night, Sara thought hollowly, feeling a sudden coldness. If Beth came this evening that would make three nights running, although she was forced to admit that previously it had only been for coffee, not dinner.

She heard Jill asking, "Will John Finley be taking us across as usual on his boat?"

"He wants to go himself, so he's taking us," Hugh replied, as he glanced at his watch.

Sara's eyes strayed to the fine gold watch strapped to his strong brown wrist as she considered the undue haste with which Jill had changed the subject when Hugh mentioned the ball. Was it, she wondered, because Jill wasn't going? Her own mind shied nervously away from the moment when he must discover that she was going herself with Ian McKenzie.

Ian had been in touch with her again only that

morning, and reluctantly she had agreed to accompany him, having run out of logical excuses. In a way she was rather looking forward to it, and couldn't really account for her state of indecision. Unless it was fear of Hugh's ambiguous remarks?

At Fionnphort, six miles from Bunessan, they met John Finley, a man quite a bit older than Hugh, who took them to Iona in a small boat powered by an outboard motor.

"He came here a few years ago," Jill whispered as the two men talked. "He's a sort of writer. Documentaries and autobiographies, that sort of thing. Nothing very financially rewarding. He stayed in a cottage like Colin's when he first came, and then purchased an old derelict property. Hugh happened to be around at the time and, to cut a long story short, helped him turn it into a habitable dwelling. And now whenever we want to take a short trip he insists on obliging. Only don't tell Hugh that I told you. He doesn't like me talking about it."

"I see . . ." Sara frowned as she leaned over the side of the boat, watching it cleave through the blue waters. Hugh Fraser was a strangely complex man. Her head turned, her eyes drawn against her will to his dark profile. Even in repose there was a cynical line to his mouth, yet he would go out of his way to help a complete stranger. The hard-headed business man, yet with some strange power to move her. Something inside him which seemed to reach out and hold her by steel-like invisible bonds. Her own response was too disturbing to contemplate easily, and she looked away, giving all her attention to the fast growing island.

The Sound was narrow, and once across they quickly dropped anchor by the jetty. Hugh quirked a friendly eyebrow at Sara as he helped her off the gently rocking boat. "If you're interested in statistics," he said briefly, glancing at her sparkling wind-flushed face, "Iona is three miles long by one wide, and about a hundred people live here."

Once away from the jetty they walked through the village to the cathedral. The village itself was quiet, most of the day visitors having already gone. Hugh, tall and dark, walked slightly behind the two girls pointing out places of particular interest, linking them briefly with authentic pieces of history.

Sara couldn't take it all in. "I'll never remember the half of what you've told us," she smiled wryly, her eyes alight as she gazed around. "I'll have to buy a guidebook, I'm afraid."

"You can certainly do that," he agreed amiably. "But you'll find plenty of books relating to Iona in the library at Lochgoil. It makes fascinating reading."

Jill started trailing behind, managing to look completely bored. "I've been here before," she grumbled, when Sara asked what was wrong.

"Once!" Hugh retorted, glancing impatiently at her glum face before Sara could reply. "And you could come here a hundred times and still find something you hadn't seen before."

"But it's all so old!" Jill protested indignantly. "And you know I never did care much for history at school, or anywhere else, for that matter! Take that graveyard, for instance . . ." She pointed an imperious finger to the graveyard of Oran, who was one of St Columba's disciples. "Forty-eight kings of Scotland are buried there, along with four of Ireland and eight of Norway. Uncle David never tired of reciting the numbers to me when I was a child. That's how I remember so well. My mind boggles even to think of it!"

Her expression was so comical that Hugh seemed to smile in spite of himself, but Sara wasn't surprised when soon afterwards Jill announced that she would rather go and see if she could find someone to talk to at the hotel.

"I'll see you there later," she said with a careless wave of her hand.

John Finley was spending the afternoon with a friend who had recently come to live on the island. Hugh explained this as he and Sara went on alone, approaching the cathedral along the Street of the Dead, along which kings and chiefs were borne for burial.

The beauty of the cathedral took Sara unawares, and her pulse-beats quickened. Unlike Jill, she had always been receptive to the beauty and atmosphere of old buildings, and her first sight of the cathedral with the sun revealing the sparkling rosiness of the granite held her spellbound.

"It's quite impressive, don't you think?" Hugh watched her face keenly as he took her arm.

As she nodded silently he smiled slightly, urging her gently on, his dark face thoughtful.

"I've never seen anything quite like it before," she confessed, finding her voice, too aware of the steely strength of his fingers through the thin material of her shirt.

They went in through the main doorway of the cathedral which he told her dated from A.D. 1500, and paused beside the tenth-century Celtic cross of St Martin with its tall stone shaft richly carved with pictures of Daniel in the lions' den, and numerous other well-known Biblical figures.

Behind the cross they went to the tiny chapel of

St Columba, believed to be built on the site of his own cell. Sara liked the idea of the undying light burning inside, but like Hugh, didn't much care for the naked electric bulb.

"What a pity it couldn't take a more authentic form," she remarked, regarding it doubtfully as they passed on through the west door into the nave.

"It would look better," he agreed, guiding her from one place of interest to another. On the Norman east wall he drew her attention to a superb oil-painting by Le Maître of Christ crucified. Although the north transept was dimly lit, there was no mistaking its quality.

What a pity, Sara thought idly, as she gazed entranced, that Colin wasn't with them this afternoon. This magnificent painting, the cathedral, the whole concept, would surely have appealed to his artistic nature.

Hugh instantly, subtly, sensed her shifting mood. "What is it, Sara?" His gaze turned on her with a hint of irony, a curious invasion of the senses which she strove to reject.

"Nothing . . ." Skilfully she evaded an answer, pushing back tendrils of hair from her hot brow as she turned too quickly from the painting and walked through the north door into the cloister. Feeling rather foolish, she stopped beside a large bronze sculpture of the Virgin Mary, which she noted nervously was modern, and erected there in 1959. She felt Hugh closing in behind her.

"Such a pity you can't bear to tell me what's bothering you, Sara. Am I such an ogre?"

"Of course not." Her pulse jerked. "I've never thought so." She urged herself to greater effort. "This afternoon you're being very kind."

His eyes were suddenly hard and mocking again. "So well said, but somehow I'm not convinced. There was definitely something, my little coward!"

She stood staring at him, half in, half out of the shadows, poised warily, almost on the verge of flight, her eyes not meeting his, fixed on the deeply shadowed cleft of his chin.

There was a moment's silence, then he said almost grimly, "Well, since you appear to have lost your tongue, and I seem to have exhausted my supply of information, we might as well go and try to find Jill. At least she never appears to be lost for words."

She was silent, waiting for the turmoil inside her to lessen, as reluctantly she left the cathedral and they walked back through the village to the hotel.

"In any case," he added, more evenly as she stumbled before him, "I think you've seen enough for one day. If you try to take in more, you might only get mental indigestion. We can always come back."

Soon after they finished tea Hugh suggested that they went for a short walk down the island to Sandeels Bay until it was time to meet John Finley.

Jill, pleading tiredness, preferred to stay and talk to some young students who were staying at the hotel, and Hugh, mindful of her recent operation, agreed.

Sara and he went alone. Sara, eager to see as much of Iona as possible in the hour they had left, thought it would be silly to miss such an opportunity, even if it did provide him with the occasional chance of taunting her whenever she said or did anything foolish. She must learn not to take any notice!

The road ran south, close to a sandy shore, its inland side flanked by crofts. It didn't go any farther than a place called the Big Strand, but as it was ebb tide they were able to walk over the sands a few hundred yards to Sandeels Bay.

The bay was small and extremely beautiful, the terrace sloping in runs below a big cliff thickly covered with ivy. The top of the cliff was capped with heather which would bloom pink as the year advanced. The whole spot was absolutely deserted, which surprised Sara. She had imagined, that there would be other tourists about.

The bay curved deeply, the white sands dazzled, and the rocks she saw were silvered with lichen. Rock pools beckoned, full of delicate, many-hued seaweeds, while before them, over the green swell of sea, lay the far distant mountains of Mull their tops hazed by pale grey cloud. The air was pure and very light, and there was a clarity of colour on Iona which seemed to invade even her seas.

Sara, almost forgetting Hugh for the moment, knelt down to remove her canvas shoes before starting to roll up the wide bottoms of her slacks. She was unprepared, and put out a startled hand to stop herself from tumbling over, when he drew her abruptly but silently into the cover of the rock.

"If you wait here for a second," he said quietly, disregarding her startled glance, "before you start paddling around in those pools, we might see some oyster-catchers. I promised to take you bird-watching, didn't I?"

Despite the heat and a day full of adventure, she felt a stir of excitement, even while she detected a teasing note in his voice and a mocking gleam in his eyes. If he considered that half an hour on a sandy beach settled his birdwatching obligations—well, who was she to argue?

There might be something here of value to Colin

Brown, although why he should keep coming to her mind she didn't know. She supposed the answer lay in her subconscious anxiety about Jill, along with her own quite genuine interest in his job.

"Look!" Hugh nudged her gently, seconds later, as several oyster-catchers settled on the beach not far away. "They're probably looking for crabs. If you sit quite still we might see one catch one."

Sara tried to do as he said, but the confined space bothered her. They were caught in a deep cleft of rock, his shoulder almost touching her own. Sand trickled through her bare toes, a curiously sensuous feeling, and her heart was beating much faster than it should be. Soon he might notice it. With a small sigh of desperation she turned her head towards the shore.

The birds, she saw, were bulky, black and white with deep bills of orange-red, and emitted a peculiar sharp *kleep*, and at times, when they were agitated, about something a rather frenzied piping sound. Noisy and seemingly sociable, they dug in sea pools with three-inch bills amongst the seaweed with some success. One seemed to catch a particularly large crab, but lost its catch to a herring gull which alighted beside it.

"May the best man win," Hugh exclaimed lazily, as the birds flew off on a noisy foray.

"Doesn't he always?" Sara retorted idly, as she groped for her sandals, her interest in the birds, and even the sea disappearing. It was time to go.

"I'd like to think so." He leaned back indolently against the rock, blocking her escape route, obviously in no hurry. "But it doesn't always happen. Women, I've found, are contrary creatures. They can develop obsessions for a man's weaknesses, and are often blind to his lack of sterner qualities."

Sara looked at him quickly. Was he referring to

137

anyone in particular? Cautiously she said, "You may be right." Bending forward, she ran her slim fingers through the fine sand, her hair clouding her face, hiding her expression. She wouldn't argue. Why end such a perfect day on a note of dissension?

But her intuition proved right when he asked abruptly, "Do you think Jill still hankers after her artist?"

Sara had a theory that if one constantly looks for disaster it is sure to arrive. This, then, was such a moment! How glad she was that because of her hair he could not see her startled reaction, or did his sharp eye notice the tensing of her fingers in the sand? How could she answer without straying too far from the truth?

As she hesitated painfully, she felt his eyes scrutinize her face and said quickly, "She probably does. I should think it more than likely."

"She hasn't confided in you?"

"Why not talk to her yourself, Hugh?"

His black brows shot up. "You're being deliberately evasive!" His words stung like gravel chips. She could never hope to fool him completely.

"Sara!"

At his brief exclamation her head came up with a jerk. So near that she could see the sharp lines about his mouth before she looked straight into his eyes. "Hugh . . ." Faintly she was aware that she used his name freely. "When Jill's mother returns wouldn't you reconsider and meet this man? He must surely have some redeeming qualities?"

His gaze slid down her bare arm, and his hand went out, gently releasing her clenched fingers one by one. His touch alarmed her, leaving fine needles of fire.

He said softly, his eyes swinging narrowly back to her pale face, "You really think I should, Sara?"

Her breath came unevenly. Was he really relenting, or was his mood transient, born from the unreality of a moment when they might be existing in another world?

Her reply came, barely audible. "I don't think you would regret it." Her voice held a faint note of wistfulness.

"Such optimism!" he mocked gently. "But for you, Sara, I might do just this one thing."

Her face glowed suddenly from an inner warmth which spread through her body. Yet she shook her head. "Whatever you do, Hugh, you must do for Jill. She has the problem, not me."

"But you could have, sooner than you think. A problem of your very own."

He spoke lazily again, enigmatically, stretching his long legs lithely beside her, curling around one finger a strand of her long fair hair.

Her heart lurched unhappily as his gaze travelled over her. Until he released her she could not break free, and, she felt, it would be foolish to beg. What had he meant by his statement? she wondered. She had experienced his ruthlessness. What would he do if he discovered that Colin was actually living here, and that she had known? It didn't bear thinking about!

Seeking distraction from her tortured nerves, she said, "Jill can't understand why her mother went to America without her."

"Better that she shouldn't." His eyes were discouraging and slightly wary.

"That sounds ominous." The words were scarcely out before she regretted them. He would think she was probing.

Suddenly he grinned. With deliberate cruelty he tugged the strand of hair, and as she winced said smoothly, "Does it now, my little curiosity? I suppose Jill put you up to this? Well, just tell her I refused to talk, and see what she makes of that."

Colour flamed wildly under Sara's skin with a kind of helpless anger. "Why be so hypocritical?"

"I'm not where you're concerned." He moved nearer and her eyes widened. "In other circumstances your beauty might have tempted me. I'm only a man."

"So long as you're not sure about it!" Irrationally, she hated that ambiguous 'might'.

His free hand shot out, catching her chin, almost bruising the delicate skin on her face as he forced her to look at him.

"All my life," he drawled, "I've done things in a hurry, but sometimes a man likes to take his time. Your air of innocence acts as a brake, but it could be wholly deceptive."

She gasped as a swift rage threatened to choke her. Her hand shot out, contacting his hard cheek as she twisted away from him in the sand, but he was too quick for her. He uncoiled like a panther, and his arms caught her as they fell together against the bank.

She had no time to catch her breath as his arms locked around her, firm as whipcord, and not to be denied. Even as she struggled, with a smothered exclamation his mouth came down on hers, salty and rough with sea air, totally without mercy. Her hands came up against his chest, trying to thrust him away, then stilled by the shock of pleasure which flooded every nerve of her slim taut body.

She couldn't move, he held her so closely, his heart beating heavily against her own. Her blood was on fire and she only wanted the moment to go on for ever, careless of his hurting lips and hands.

There could be other forms of punishment, but none so devastating as this. The air seemed filled with the song of the oyster-catchers, but she was past caring. His mouth burnt as the minutes slowed and lengthened, until the bruising pressure eased and he lifted his dark head, staring narrowly down at her flushed face.

Then suddenly she was pushing away from him, her thoughts chaotic, but knowing as she did so a primitive urge to be back in his arms.

Her voice shook as she looked at him wildly. "Is this your usual form of chastisement?" On her lips she could still taste the saltiness of his.

His eyes, curiously intent, stayed on her bruised mouth before going to her thickly fringed blue eyes, still clouded with emotion. He mocked deliberately, "I couldn't think of anything more charming."

She drew back, an involuntary motion of protest. "I didn't enjoy it," she retorted fiercely, as he looked down at her, a definite hint of a threat in his eyes.

He said softly, "You're the hypocrite now, or didn't you know it?"

Carefully Sara raised herself to a sitting position. "You advised me to seek a romantic attachment."

"You wouldn't find it such a shattering experience with Ian McKenzie. You could probably cope."

"Whatever do you mean?"

His lip curled derisively. "Do you want me to explain?"

"No—I—" Sara's lips trembled so that she could scarcely force words through them, as she shrank from having her emotions laid bare in front of her. She stared up into his darkly handsome face. He had some hold over her. Some part of her responded unpredictably to his dominant personality. If she didn't fight

141

she could be utterly subdued and crushed, and she was suddenly afraid.

"We'd better go," she finished helplessly, thrusting back her heavy hair with shaking fingers.

"So help me!" he muttered, staring at her savagely. "Haven't you ever been kissed before? Or will you try to deny it?" His head came up abruptly.

"I think I hate you," she retorted, knowing otherwise, trying to ignore the tearing pain inside her.

"So you keep saying." She flinched from the smooth satire in his voice. "But I think you know it's not true, and I think I could prove it." His eyes dwelt on her softly curved lips. "You might even enjoy the experience, in fact I would even guarantee it. Only I must admit you're not quite what I'm used to."

"Which hasn't seemed much of an impediment so far," she raged. "But I'm certainly not one of your women from the desert, or some tropical jungle!" With her temper came a small measure of composure which slowed her racing pulse.

There was a flare of amusement in his eyes as they glinted on the erratic nerve at the base of her throat. "What wouldn't I do with you in the jungle, Sara! You wouldn't escape me there."

She knew he laughed at her, but his eyes were the dark smouldering grey of steel, and she felt the awful weakness of fascination. She had acknowledged before that she was no match for him verbally, and a transient hope that she might outwit him in another way died gently in her breast. Her folly lay in attempting the impossible.

She shook her head, sadly bereft of words, as he jumped to his feet, moving quickly for so big a man.

"We'd better get out of here," Hugh said soberly, his jesting gone as he jerked her up and towards him in one supple lithe movement, his fingers hurting her wrist. "With your hair loose, and," his eyes travelled downwards, "your feet bare, I won't be responsible if we stay any longer."

With a shrug he released her as she stared at him, fighting the feather sensation inside her, her eyes huge in her pale face.

She bent automatically to pick up her sandals, feeling slightly sick with an unexplainable humiliation, longing to be away from him. She said, her voice quite without expression, "Don't worry, it won't happen again."

He laughed at that, a cynical sound, his eyes full of unspoken derision as they turned to walk silently back along the shore.

They returned to Lochgoil, and chaos, later that evening. It seemed that Biddy, after a disagreement with Jean, had insisted that she had been in bed long enough, and would get up and cook dinner herself. Katie, unduly alarmed, had decided to ring Dr McKenzie and he had arrived at the same time as Beth. As he had still been there when they returned from Iona, Hugh could do no less than ask him to stay for the evening, an offer which had been accepted with unashamed alacrity.

"Presumably he needs to keep an eye on the invalid," Hugh murmured drily, for Sara's ears alone, as they sat down at the table.

Sara winced, ignoring his sally as he pushed in her chair. Did he not miss a thing? Ian's eyes had been on her almost constantly since she had come downstairs five minutes ago. He would have been sitting beside her now if Hugh hadn't neatly, and, she thought, deliberately forestalled him.

"I trust Biddy is able to carry on?" Hugh caustically addressed the doctor as he took a seat opposite between Jill and Beth—a Beth who was looking particularly attractive in a smart black dress.

"I should think so." Ian's grey-blue eyes, not without a sense of humour, twinkled. "It would certainly have been better if she'd stayed in bed a little longer, but one can't work miracles. Sara has done wonders to keep her off her feet for a week, and she's promised to take things easy."

"She can't bear the thought of anyone else in her kitchen," Beth retorted crisply with raised eyebrows. "So you must just humour her, Hugh darling."

"Perhaps if Hugh decides to stay and get married, his wife might cope with her," said Jill, with a poker face, greatly daring. "I just can't deal with Biddy's tantrums."

"My wife's could be much worse," Hugh teased suavely, glancing with some amusement at Jill as he filled Ian's wine glass.

"I shouldn't think so!" Jill laughed as she picked up her soup spoon. "Mummy says you always choose well—for a man."

"I wonder . . ."

Sara felt suddenly slightly ill as she toyed with the food on her plate, unwilling to look up, her head spinning. In the muted glow from the centre light she looked almost ethereal, her dress with its soft swirling patterns clinging to her slender figure with innocent provocation. She was too conscious of Hugh by her side, a distracting element with his strange magnetism which she seemed unable to resist.

Her peculiar lassitude she put down to tiredness and the emotional excitement of the afternoon. The sensation of sea and sky, the subtlety of sun shimmering on water was still with her, emphasizing the disturbing reality of the moment. Hugh had parried Jill's remarks about a wife almost as if he had already made up his mind.

She knew a sense of relief when Beth, with a frowning stare in Jill's direction, started talking about Iona, asking numerous sharp questions about their day.

Ian leaned carefully forward, saying to Sara, his eyes faintly reproachful. "If I'd known you wanted to go there, I'd have been delighted to take you. In fact I have to go next week to see a patient, if you'd care to go again?"

"Oh, I'm sorry . . ." She stared at him uncertainly. Nothing that had happened since they had returned had been able to obliterate the magic of Iona. But, in retrospect, she forced herself to concentrate on the cathedral rather than Sandeels Bay. She couldn't bear to go back again, not straight away. But how to refuse? Already she had discovered that Ian could be stubbornly perverse.

Hugh said hardly as she hesitated, "Sara happens to be a working girl, Ian. I can't spare her, I'm afraid. Not with the pressure of work here. Today was an exception. I wanted to see John Finley, and thought it would be a change for Jill."

"And I want her for a day myself," Jill inserted quickly before Ian could protest. "I thought we might go to Oban as I want a dress for the ball. I haven't a single thing to wear."

Sara shot her a puzzled glance. Only this morning Jill had declared that she wasn't going to Beth's dance. Why the sudden change of mind? Furthermore, if Jill had decided that there wasn't anything suitable amongst the array of dresses in her wardrobe, then what about her own? Sara had brought very little in the way of party dresses to Lochgoil. Of course some women must have something new for every occasion. But during the few days she had been here Jill hadn't given the impression that she was one of those. More than likely she just wanted another day out.

Hugh moved irritably by her side. "Why on earth didn't you bring a dress with you, Jill? You might have known you would need it."

Jill smiled sweetly at her brother, her eyes wide and guileless. "My operation, dear Hugh! I felt too ill to even think about the dance, so don't be mean about Sara. I'm sure you can spare her for a few hours. Don't you agree, Ian?" She turned her pleading face towards the doctor.

Ian nodded, momentarily in league with her, his good humour restored. "At any rate," he grinned, "I'm taking Sara to the ball. You can't possibly work her through that, old man."

While everyone chuckled Sara found it difficult to raise a smile, and in a curious fashion her eyes gravitated to Hugh, noticing with sudden nervous apprehension that his mouth had drawn into a tight line.

His eyes glittered narrowly at the smiling man across the table, yet he said carelessly, with little sign of anger, "I'll say this for you, McKenzie, you don't waste much time. Unless," he added smoothly, "you're being a trifle presumptuous?"

Sara stirred uneasily, twirling the stem of her wine glass, her fingers taut as he turned his head. His hard dark eyes encountered hers, and there was unconcealed cynicism in their depth. She knew it was up to her to say something, but she didn't know how to answer and moved her shoulders in a helpless gesture.

"It was only arranged yesterday morning," she confessed unhappily, glancing at Beth. "Miss Asquith asked me too, the other day, and I didn't think you would mind."

"Hugh probably imagines I'll run away with you," Ian laughed, his pleasant face beaming, obviously not aware of any particular undercurrents. His gaze lingered enthusiastically on Sara's pink cheeks. "I haven't been able to get to the ball for years, owing to the nature of my work, but nothing short of a catastrophe is going to stop me this time."

And that, Sara decided, as the conversation became general once more, seemed to be that!

But later, just before he went home, as Sara was having a last word with him about Biddy, Ian entreated her again not to forget that she had promised to go out with him.

"It's not that the ball is so important, Sara, you know that." His nice eyes were suddenly serious. "I've never met a girl like you before. I think I'm falling in love."

"Oh, please, Ian . . ." Startled, Sara stared up at him. "You can't be serious! You've only known me a few days." A state of confusion blended with tiredness jangled her nerves. He looked so sincere, almost as if he believed what he was saying. If only she wasn't so completely aware of another man, how very different everything might be. A wave of despair swamped logical thought, and she could only look at Ian mutely.

But before she could say anything more, with a rueful grin he picked up his old tweed cap and turned towards the door, almost as if he guessed a little of what she was thinking. "Never mind, sleep on it, Sara. Don't let it worry you now." With a gentle touch of his hand he was gone, leaving her gazing after him.

It had certainly been quite a day!

CHAPTER EIGHT

JILL decided not to go to Oban after all for a new dress. It had, she confessed to Sara, been a hasty decision born from a sudden urge to spend a whole day with Colin, who might have gone with them. But, after some thought, she had come to the definite conclusion that the risk wasn't worth taking.

"Hugh might easily find out," she sighed. "Or he might have insisted on coming with me himself in case I have a relapse or something. And you know what he is. He has eyes in the back of his head!"

Sara smiled wryly at Jill's quip. She had no inclination to go shopping for clothes with Jill. Nor had she any real desire to leave Lochgoil, even for a day, and she could only feel distinctly relieved that the girl had changed her mind.

They were sitting on the terrace in the garden after tea. The warm spring sunshine had enticed them out, and with Biddy active once more Sara found she had more time on her hands. She stretched luxuriously and turned her face up to the sun.

Jill stirred restlessly when Sara made no reply. She didn't care for silence of any kind. Her eyes roamed thoughtfully over Sara's pale profile.

"I heard Hugh telling Beth the other night that he might be going down to London again next week. I might go with him for a couple of days, if he'll have me. Colin has quite a lot of work to catch up on, and I'd only be in the way and make him irritable. Whereas if I go with Hugh he can forget all about me until I come back."

Sara turned her head slowly and stared at her, startled out of her inertia. "Mr Fraser didn't mention it, and we've been busy in the office all morning."

"Probably never thought of it," Jill shrugged. "He's much too busy running after Beth. I don't know why I worry so much about keeping Colin out of sight. I don't suppose he'd notice if the two of us sat on top of Ben More!"

"You were only saying a minute ago that he never misses a thing, or words to that effect?"

"Must you always take me so literally!" Jill's eyebrows rose impatiently. "I'm only trying to point out that sometimes love seems to make people blind. He's almost sure to announce his engagement at the dance."

"You mean—to Beth?" Sara tried to smile, but her lips only stretched painfully.

"Who else?" Jill hesitated only slightly before rushing on. "I've been watching them closely and I'm sure there are signs."

"Signs?" Mystified, Sara frowned, her eyes intent on Jill's face, unable to stop herself from asking the question.

Idly Jill's fingers went on pulling the white petals from some daisies which she had found on the lawn. She loved to talk at any time, and especially when she had an audience that seemed to be hanging on her every word as Sara was.

"It doesn't take good eyesight, or foresight, or what have you, to see," she remarked smugly. "I've put two and two together! Hugh's thinking of staying at Lochgoil, as I've told you before. Well, now it seems that he's ordered two puppies from a breeder on the mainland, and he has plans to start breeding ponies.

He's always been interested in horses, you see. And on top of this, I believe he intends to build some new cottages on the estate as some of the old ones are in a very bad state of repair, almost past converting. So taking everything into consideration, Beth should be pleased!"

"Pleased?" Sara echoed carefully, taking off her sun-glasses and placing them neatly on the wooden garden table by her side. "How do you mean, she's pleased? You could be mistaken..." She swallowed the constriction in her throat. "Hugh might actually have decided to leave Lochgoil altogether, and sell the castle after he's tidied it up a bit. Beth might not want to live here at all."

"I think you're mistaken," Jill retorted, losing interest in the daisies which she flung with final cruelty into the garden pool. "Anyway," she shrugged vaguely, "time will tell. And, by the way," she turned her sharply derisive eyes from the pool to Sara again, "why all the 'Mr Frasers' this afternoon? Yesterday, when we came back from Iona, it was Hugh. In fact if Beth hadn't been around, and you'd been any other than his secretary, I might have thought he was quite taken with you, darling Sara."

"Don't be silly! Sometimes I do call Mr Fraser Hugh." Confused, Sara jumped to her feet, flushing scarlet. Jill was impossible! She moved restlessly, a sudden urge to get away from the castle overwhelming her. It was pleasant in the garden, but somehow she felt unable to sit any longer, dwelling on what Jill had just told her.

"Would you mind, Jill," she pleaded, "if I borrowed your Mini for a couple of hours? I feel like having a walk somewhere, probably on Ben More. I've spent the whole afternoon in the cottage with

Gwen, so I could do with some fresh air. Please tell Biddy not to keep dinner for me. I'll just have a snack when I get back."

"Okay, my pet." Jill waved her hand carelessly. "But I don't know how you can be bothered. I'm going to take a long hot bath myself. Then after dinner I'm taking Katie down to Salen to see her aunt, so I won't be needing you any more tonight."

Sara smiled, against her better judgement, at the regal note in Jill's voice. She knew exactly what Jill would do. She would drop Katie off at Miss Black's cottage, then go on to spend the evening with Colin.

However, she made no comment, apart from murmuring briefly, "I'll see you tomorrow, then."

For her there was no satisfaction to be gained from the excitement of secret meetings and deceiving Hugh. She shivered suddenly as she turned away. She was constantly aware of the deception she practised, and the knowledge weighed heavily. Her nerves, she knew, were stretched almost to breaking point, but it hadn't seemed to matter so much until these last few days. Now, although at times he didn't seem aware of her existence, she was constantly aware of him and the tumult he could raise inside her. Much of what had happened between them had been entirely her own fault, and she had only herself to blame if talk of his engagement to another girl hurt. No man regarded a few kisses seriously, but even so she longed to feel his arms around her again, even if it had to be in a mood of antagonistic reaction.

"Don't worry about hurrying back," Jill called as she came downstairs with a cardigan. "I can always take the Land-Rover."

Perhaps she should have taken it herself, Sara thought, as she drove down the side of Loch na Keal.

The setting was beautiful, the weather more so. May and June in the Highlands could be beautiful, with long hours of daylight and sunshine, and a dry warmth which banished from the mind the wild cold days of winter.

Carefully she slowed down, looking for a suitable place to park. Clouds built up from the west, changing the colour of the loch perpetually, from muted greys to blues more brilliant than many of the Mediterranean seas she had seen on holiday during recent years.

She stopped the car and sat for a moment before getting out. The skies here were wide, the land open. For months of the year the islands might be ravaged by rain and desolation, but never gloom. Yet there was a certain starkness which instilled a pang of misgiving in Sara's heart. At close quarters the bare hanging rock, the lonely waste of brown land, could give an impression of unmitigated bleakness.

In spite of the involuntary shudder that ran through her, Sara found that she didn't really mind the bleakness. Today, it seemed to find an answering echo in her own heart. The sun came hot on her head, but she took her cardigan from the car. Up here, as Hugh said, temperatures could change with alarming suddenness.

With a feeling of exhilaration slightly shifting her mood of depression, she started off over the rough moor. She found a stream—a burn it would be called in these parts, she supposed—and watched it trickling over the stones on its rocky bed before stooping to scoop a handful of the clear cool water to her dry lips. Farther on she removed her cardigan, then crouching on a rocky outcrop of the burn she took a handful of small stones and carefully spelt out her first name, laying the stones in close formation, a frown of concentration creasing her smooth brow.

When she had been a child her mother had sometimes played with her by the small stream near their Welsh home. It had been a game, spelling out their names, racing to see who could be finished first. Her mother's name had been Emma, four letters, the same as her own, so there had been no handicap. Looking back, it didn't take a lot of imagination to see why she had usually been allowed to win, but to Sara, then a five-year-old, the winning of the simplest game had been a huge victory.

A sigh escaped her as she continued on her way, following the sparkling water until the sight of a young deer standing on a crag diverted her. There could be more. Carefully she approached, but the deer, alert and wary, nervously threw back its head, spotted her coming and ran off. There didn't appear to be any more.

Slowly, staring, half dreaming in the still warm sunshine, Sara wandered on, letting the silence and the pine-scented air lull her into a state of almost drugged tranquillity. She left the burn and went to sit on the sheltered side of a rock-strewn boulder before returning to the road. Already she had come a little way up Ben More. It was known to be a fairly easy mountain to climb, but not without a map and compass. She knew these to be essential. However, she hadn't set out to climb. She only sought to tire herself out physically, to get away from her thoughts. And as she sat down with her back against the warm rock she seemed to have achieved just that.

Out in the distance a hawk hovered in space, its wings vibrating through the stillness, hypnotic to watch. Sara watched until her heavy eyelids fell.

There was only the hawk and the sun, and the wind sighing. Soon she was fast asleep.

It was as simple as that. Afterwards she couldn't remember the moment, nor what woke her up, unless it was a sort of built-in warning system which operated even while she slept. For a frightening space of time she couldn't even remember where she was. A suspended moment of a nightmare, with no clues to be derived from the thick blanket of fog all around her. She could well have been in another world, or half-way between two planets. Never had she seen such cotton wool whiteness, such a thickness of air, which to her frightened eyes appeared solid and impenetrable.

After what seemed an eternity she moved, though only very slowly and carefully, scarcely daring to break the eerie silence. Silence, such as she had never known before, although she seemed to remember reading a poem about it. Something about the Hebrides, and the silence of the seas. With a wry smile she wondered if the poet had ever been stuck like this.

Her flash of humour seemed to dispel a little of her fear and she scrambled to her feet. Cramp shot through one leg as she glanced at her watch, stabbing her with pain so that she winced on a quickly indrawn breath. It was almost eight o'clock. She must have slept well over an hour. As the pain eased, panic replaced it. Tragic stories of people lost on mountains flooded her head. Her father had been a member of a mountain rescue team once, and she knew that they didn't always get there in time.

Rather desperately she tried to remember some of the rules. She must stay put. This was the first thing. Not to do anything foolish so as to risk falling over a precipice before help arrived. Help? Sara sat down again, huddled in a small heap. This started off another devastating train of thought. Help could only arrive, if it ever did, in the form of Hugh Fraser! He would be the only one to know. Jill would mention where she had gone, and when she didn't come back ... Thoughts of his reactions swirled her brain into ice-cold chasms. She had been foolish, but he wouldn't describe it that way. His temper, she knew from experience, was uncertain, and she shuddered to think what he would say if he found her like this. She could only pray that the mist would clear so that she could find her own way back before such a contingency arose.

Impatiently she pushed back her heavy hair and tried to take stock. Her clothes, she realized, were totally inadequate for a night in the open, but her position was sheltered and fairly warm, almost as if the heat of the day had been trapped in the rock. Apart from discomfort, she would probably take little harm until morning if the mist didn't clear and no one came. Hastily she thrust from her mind frightening thoughts of the lonely darkness yet to come. All she must do was to listen quietly and be ready to answer if someone called.

According to her watch she had only waited half an hour before she heard the shout, but to Sara, sitting beside the rock, it seemed more like days.

That was how Hugh found her, crouched beneath the lofty crag, shivering. Sara didn't hear him until he stood, almost on top of her.

"You must have been born under a lucky star," he said soberly, as she gazed up at him, her face pale and immobile, her eyes wide with a curious mixture of fear and gratitude.

The damp cardigan clung to her thin body, and her heart raced with a sudden rush of emotion as his eyes flicked her defenceless face.

"How did you find me?" she gasped, unable to get up because her legs trembled so. "I didn't shout."

"Well, I did," his eyes glittered, "and if you'd been listening and answered, I might have been here sooner. It could have been a help."

She shook her head mutely, "I'm sorry," she murmured at last, her voice unsteady. "I'm afraid I didn't hear you." Her hands were clenched so tightly that the knuckles were white. She could see from the set of his head that he was in a dangerous mood.

He still towered above her, giving nothing away. "I found your name at the burn," he said, his face expressionless, "and that of your mother. Your friend in London talked of her as Emma. It put me on the right track, but I was just about to give up when I stumbled across you. As it is I was crazy to come so far on my own."

"So far?" Sara choked. What did he mean?

"Far enough." He stared tersely, his eyes darkening. "You must have wandered miles."

It didn't seem possible, but she didn't dare protest as he crouched down beside her, his head bent towards her. "Didn't you realize the danger of wandering around a place like this by yourself, without any equipment, not even a proper coat. If I hadn't been able to find you, you could have been frozen stiff long before morning, dressed as you are now."

His eyes ran over her lightly clad body boldly, and she shook like a leaf in a storm. His voice was torn between exasperation and concern. "It wasn't really worth it, was it?"

Her sharp little indrawn breath was quite audible

in the fraught air. "You think I did this deliberately?"

"Perhaps. Some people enjoy being rescued." His dark face swam above her, coolly ironic, sharpening the pain in her breast.

Quick stabbing darts of anger were piercing her. "I can't prove anything," she whispered vehemently. "You'll just have to take my word for it."

Cynicism touched his clearly defined mouth, "We're all apt to be misjudged," he commented drily.

She stared at him, suspended in a strange void. Angry words rushed to her lips, but she could say nothing. Could he be right? Could she possibly have come up here hoping subsconsciously that he would come after her? If only she could get away from his sceptical eyes and find a hole to crawl into! He must be offering fervent thanks for women like Beth Asquith, who had probably never done anything so foolish in her life.

"Even if it was true . . ." he watched her closely, "you obviously don't understand how dangerous a mountain can be."

"You put it so baldly. I didn't even think of getting lost!"

"What did you expect?"

She started to struggle unsteadily to her feet with a jerky movement away from him, but his lean brown hand descended with enough force on her shoulder to hold her quite still.

"You may as well stay where you are." He gave a slight, scarcely perceptible shrug. "I don't know about you, but I'm not risking my own neck twice. We could as easily take the wrong track as the right. As I said before, I must have been crazy to come up here by myself."

A million prickles ran over her skin as she tried

to pull away from that hard hand. The mocking quirk to his mouth actually hurt her. She gave him a swift imploring glance as he dropped down beside her, his strong boots clattering on the rough stony ground.

He relented slightly, his eyes flickering over their position with brief appraisal. "We'll wait here for a while. Maybe the mist will clear. The wind's rising a bit, and the forecast's good. With any luck it could be gone in half an hour. We're a fair way up the mountain, but not nearly to the top."

She was shaken and stared at him, a faintly perplexed expression on her face. "Won't they be worrying at Lochgoil?"

He flexed his shoulders against the rock, seeking a comfortable spot as he released her with a careless gesture. "I told them to give me until ten. With any luck we'll make it, it's only after eight. If not, with any luck, we might get help."

"I'm surprised you don't throw me over a precipice," she said in a rush, almost recklessly.

He smiled ironically, his gaze on her hot cheeks. "I assure you I don't abandon my responsibilities so lightly. Even supposing I could find a precipice."

She evaded his eyes, turning away blindly, looking out at the gathering darkness, asking inconsequently, "Have you had dinner?"

"In the kitchen," he drawled, "in a hurry. I'm afraid I'm not the sort of hero who goes running up mountains on an empty stomach, not even for a girl as attractive as yourself."

"I'm sorry," she said stiffly, concentrating on the darkness. How could she tell him that she had been driven out here by the strength and uncertainty of her own feelings? Knowing that he was spending the afternoon with Beth had induced a delicate kind of torture, past enduring. But better that he should think her completely irresponsible, than he should guess the depth of emotion which had tumbled her headlong into her present dilemma.

Silently he drew a small flask from his pocket and passed it to her. "Drink that." His quick eyes narrowed over her. "You're cold."

She took the flask, unwillingly, holding it in her cold hands.

"Drink it!" He looked at her intently. Her eyes were huge in her pale face, her hair disordered by the wind, a thick swirling mane about her cheeks which were smudged with brown earth.

Obediently she tilted her chin, choking a little as the fiery liquid ran down her bare throat. While she drank he brought a Thermos from his other pocket and poured hot black coffee.

"From Biddy," he said briefly, screwing the top on the whisky again as she passed it back. "I managed to consume some dinner while she fixed it up."

The whisky and coffee together had a magical effect. Warmth flooded back into Sara's body, driving out the chill, lifting her drooping spirits although the mist still swirled.

Controlling the tremor in her voice, she said softly, "I shouldn't like you to think that I'm not grateful."

"Oh, God," he groaned sardonically, "spare me that!"

She stared at him, her face utterly bewildered, puzzled by his sudden change of manner, "I'm sorry," she murmured a shade sharply.

When he made no comment she wrapped her arms around herself and huddled lower. Her face felt dirty and her shirt was rumpled with one button torn off, but she didn't much care. Her hair bothered her. She had long since lost the elastic band which held it back, and it was loose about her shoulders, the fine strands blowing across her mouth.

Impatiently she tried to thrust it back. "When I get time I'm going to have this cut! A short style would be nice and easy to manage."

His eyes slipped over her downbent head. "Don't ever do that!" His voice held soft menace. "Leave your hair as it is. I like it."

"It won't be long before I'm gone, so it can't matter." A quiver ran through her, a painful tremor, and she clasped her arms tighter, so that he shouldn't see.

He misconstrued her reaction, and instantly his mood changed. "You're still cold?"

His arm caught her, hauling her close up against him, his dark face taut. "We could be here a while, and cold can be the very devil."

Her breath caught in her throat, she tried to struggle. "Let me go!"

Instantly he gave her a terse little shake. "I don't happen to be joking, or looking for an excuse to get you in my arms. I don't want you passing out on me, that's all." His arms tightened. "Are you any warmer?"

"I'm not cold." Her face was burning beneath his mocking candour, and she hated him, with a clear cold hate.

"Then why are you trembling?" His steely fingers reached for hers, testing their temperature. "Your clothing," his voice was dry, "isn't entirely suitable."

She said, "I had my cardigan and the sun was hot."

"And now it isn't, and that cardigan is entirely inadequate." Quickly, before she could protest, he unzipped his large coat, wrapping it around her so that it encompassed them both, and she was fast against the warmth of his chest.

Unbidden, Sara felt a fever of excitement rising within her, and closed her eyes, determined that he shouldn't guess. A weight of longing came over her from nowhere, stunning her so heavily that she was afraid to move or speak.

The minutes passed slowly. "Are you feeling any better?" Hugh asked presently.

She had been dreaming, but when he spoke she glanced at him quickly, to see him looking at her a little oddly. She turned her head away abruptly, catching her breath. Her heart seemed to be beating loudly in the stillness, and the only reality was the man who was regarding her with oblique concern.

"I asked you a question!" he said sharply, when she didn't answer.

"I'm sorry." She felt her cheeks burning again. "Of course I'm feeling better. I don't need your coat."

One dark eyebrow soared. "Woman's ingratitude to man!" He surveyed her mockingly.

He lifted his hand, she thought to remove his coat, but instead he tipped her head back forcibly, his fingers smoothing the heavy hair away from her forehead, heedless of the tangles. With deliberate deftness he lifted it from her neck, running his eyes over her delicately boned face, lingering with punishing intentness on the smudges, brown against the whiteness of her cheeks, and her gold-tipped lashes.

"Hugh..." With a faint sigh she heard his name on her lips, scarcely aware that she had uttered it. There came a sudden unquestionable longing inside her, a tearing kind of hunger, not lessened by the feel of his strong body against her own. Bitter-sweet sensations began to mingle.

But he didn't move. Only his hand continued to explore her face, his gaze pinning her down, arousing emotions she hadn't been aware that she possessed.

"You were saying?" he prompted softly, his voice low against the rising wind, but faintly persuasive.

"Nothing . . ." Confusion swept over her and her heavy eyelids fell. It was the only protection she had against his ability to read her like a book. Deep colour stained her cheeks, and even in the failing light she was afraid that he would see.

There was a moment's silence when, as she had feared, his finger unerringly traced the flare of pink, and he said slowly, "You're beginning to feel again, Sara. For too long you've been determined to live on a barren, unemotional plane, but now it's receding."

The lick of flame in his voice brought her right back to her senses, but she dared not move, her body went taut. She was afraid of how much he might guess. Her barren, unemotional plane, as he called it, had been invaded by a man who almost certainly belonged to someone else. Did he expect her to feel gratitude for awakening feelings which he obviously viewed with clinical detachment? Her eyes stung with sudden rage and tears. She could feel the warmth of his skin through the thin silk of her blouse and shuddered convulsively.

But even as she tried again to thrust him away, his arms tightened, crushing her body with a soft fluid movement against his own, then abruptly his head lifted, sensing danger, scanning the sky.

"The cloud!" Alert to the elements, his gaze went over her head. "It's lifting with the wind. We'd better hurry."

He was on his feet, pulling Sara with him, concentrating on the weather, his arrogant dark head clearly etched against the night sky. The wind was rising steadily, whipping at her hair, tearing at her clothes, filling the night with noise where before there had only been an eerie silence. The mist, she saw, now only covered the top of the mountain, while around and below them the ground lay clear. But as she lifted her hot cheeks gratefully to the cooling wind, there came with it a fine drizzle of rain, and a definite threat of more to come.

"We'd better hurry," Hugh repeated, turning from his brief scan of the universe to slip out of his coat and zip it quickly around her. Quieting her feeble protests with one sharp look, he methodically picked up the Thermos before taking hold of her arm with his other hand. His terse expression brooked no argument, as he relentlessly turned her around.

"We have some way to go, and the cloud could come down again at any minute. It's that sort of night, so just start walking, there's a good girl. The next time we might not be so lucky." His mouth was grim as he slanted a quick glance at her trance-like face.

He was right, as Sara soon realized. After half an hour, and within a hundred yards of the road, they were surrounded once more by a thick penetrating fog. He pushed her none too gently ahead of him, refusing to let her stop until they reached the vehicles. Breathlessly she doubted whether she would ever have made it on her own. They seemed to have walked for miles, yet it didn't appear to have taken them very long.

"I happen to know this area well," he told her curtly. "As a boy I enjoyed climbing Ben More." A certain weariness tinged with tension ringed his mouth, as she paused for a minute in the darkness, oddly poised as if ready for flight. "I want you to promise me, Sara, that you'll never come here again by yourself."

Sara wrenched open the door of the Mini and dived in. Anything to get away from that crisp, autocratic note in his voice. He wasn't pleading or pretending a solicitude he didn't feel. All he asked was that she didn't make a nuisance of herself in this particular way again.

Rather blindly she groped for the ignition. "You're a tyrant!" she choked, not looking at him, guiltily aware that while most people would be showering him with effusive thanks, some aching part of her refused to comply. Her whole being rebelled against a fate which had allowed her to fall in love with a man to whom she meant nothing at all.

She looked up and felt her nerves shrivel with apprehension. There was something near to anger in his eyes, almost as if her tense remark stung, yet he smiled, a mocking, characteristic smile, which relegated her to the ranks of precocious children. "You were saying?" he prompted, with steely intent, his hand acting as a break on the door, his voice challenging.

"Oh, sorry . . ." With a slightly metallic laugh she decided to brazen it out. Better a discordant note than that he should guess the true state of her feelings. If she was extremely careful that final humiliation should never be hers.

She forced her eyes to meet his narrow stare, her lips parting with deliberate flippancy, "I am truly grateful, as I thought I'd said before, but if it pleases you, I'll say it again, and promise to behave myself in future, Mr Fraser."

"Which could mean anything or nothing! Take a

bow, Miss Winton." With a half smothered exclamation the car door slammed and jumped with the force of his derision, as he neatly stepped to one side and waved her on. "All I ask now is that you keep out of my way in future."

Which, Sara thought, with a frown of bewilderment, as her foot jerked on to the accelerator, seemed a very odd thing for a man to say to his secretary!

Jill said, "I don't know why Hugh was so mad because I wasn't here when you got back last night. I tried to explain that I knew he would find you, but he just wouldn't listen. I thought he was making a great fuss about nothing. After all, it was only you."

Sara hid a wry smile, disregarding Jill's outspokenness with an amused shrug. "He was probably cross about something else altogether. Your being out so late, I should imagine," she suggested mildly.

"How very stupid. I'm not a child any more!"

Stung, this time, by the tone of Jill's voice. Sara said sharply, "Apart from that, speaking generally, there could have been lives at stake. Anyone can get into difficulties, and you were supposed to get help if we didn't return."

Jill tossed her head unrepentantly. "You're quite as bad as he is. And I still say there was no need for him to be in such a temper. It was only after ten, and Katie knew where to find me."

"Katie seems to know a lot of things," Sara remarked drily. "I suppose she knew about Colin being here long before I did?"

It was Jill's turn to shrug, although she did look slightly ashamed. "Katie has been here all my life. Well, ever since I can remember," she amended, "So naturally all her loyalty lies with me. And," she added pettishly, staring at Sara, "I can rely on her."

"Fine," Sara agreed, a trifle wearily. "So you can. But do remember that we can't achieve the impossible. Hugh's bound to find out, and to be quite frank, I'll be somewhat relieved when he does. If I were you I'd just concentrate on a good explanation."

Jill threw her a sullen glance as she jumped to her feet, her curly hair awry. "For goodness' sake don't start lecturing again. I've had enough to last me a lifetime! Why on earth should Hugh object to my marrying Colin if he intends to marry a bitchy type like Beth? No one ever bothers about me!"

A quick sickness touched Sara's heart, combined with a painful drumming in her head, through which she heard herself murmuring ineffectually, "People have tried to help . . ."

"Different people choose different ways!" Jill retorted enigmatically, her cheeks pink with irritation. "But let me tell you I don't much care if Hugh does find out. In fact he could be in for a shock, and sooner than you think!"

Taking no notice of Sara's strained white face, she turned to pick up a blue wool coat from the chair in Sara's room where she had been sitting.

"Well, are you coming or are you not?" Jill's voice was still laced with impatience as she made for the door, and picking up her own coat, Sara, clearly reluctant, followed.

Jill, in one of her childishly vindictive moods, was not particularly good company, and Sara wished she hadn't agreed to her suggestion that they both had their hair done professionally for the dance. Now, it was too late to change her mind without arousing Jill's suspicions. Jill had a flair for asking awkward questions, along with a talent for extracting interesting answers. She could almost have made a career from it, Sara decided with an exasperated sigh, as she ran downstairs by her side.

In the hall they bumped into Hugh. Sara had been busy in the office all morning, following a sheet of closely written instructions which she had found lying on her desk after breakfast. Apart from a few short minutes when he had looked in to put his signature to an urgent letter, this was the first time she had seen him to speak to all day.

As he stepped to one side to let them pass his dark brows rose fractionally at the sight of their outdoor clothes.

Sara hesitated, her face flushing slightly before his brief appraisal. "You will remember, Mr Fraser," she said hesitantly, when Jill, obviously still at loggerheads with her brother, made no effort to speak, "you will remember," she repeated, "that you gave me permission to have my hair done this afternoon."

She stood there a little uncertain, while Jill walked straight on through the door.

His eyes travelled over her fair head with suave deliberation, faintly satirical. "Now you come to mention it, Miss Winton, I believe I did. And after last night you could probably do with a little cosseting, although your hair always looks beautiful to me."

From somewhere, unbidden, came the idiotic notion that he was making love to her. If it hadn't been for the faintly punishing gleam at the back of his eyes, she might have believed that her imagination wasn't just playing her tricks.

His parting words convinced her that she was being quite stupid, when he said smoothly, "This hairdresser you're going to is very clever. Beth always looks like a film star after she's been."

Outside on the drive Jill had the Mini waiting, and was tooting impatiently. The sound seemed to disperse Sara's frozen immobility. She stared up at him fixedly, then with a scarcely audible inarticulate excuse, which could have meant anything, she turned on her heels and fled.

CHAPTER NINE

LATER that same day, as she sat waiting for Ian to collect her for the ball, Sara was only aware of an increasing despair. She didn't feel like going out at all. Not even the unconcealed admiration in Ian's eyes when at last he arrived seemed able to lift her depression. How could she bear it if, as Jill thought he might, Hugh announced his engagement to Beth that evening? She thrust the thought painfully from her mind as she climbed quickly into Ian's car.

Hugh had gone on ahead with a neighbour and Jill, leaving Sara and Ian to follow. Sara had deliberately stayed in her room until they left, determined to give him no opportunity of guessing the true state of her feelings, or of making some remark which might strain beyond endurance her already precarious self-control.

Unsteadily she took a deep breath, willing herself out of her self-absorption as Ian apologized anxiously for being late.

"It doesn't matter," she smiled warmly, her blue eyes sympathetic. "I know all about such matters. No matter what happens your patients must come first."

"I expect so," he grinned wryly, glancing at her gratefully as they sped along. "Fortunately it was only a minor mishap, although that actually seemed to make me feel much worse at the time, if you know what I mean."

Sara nodded, still smiling as she looked at him. In Highland dress he looked extremely debonair, and was obviously in a good mood in spite of his setback. Surely it shouldn't be so difficult to put the image of Hugh's darkly handsome face from her mind for one evening and enjoy herself?

It was a fairly long drive to Beth's home near Carsaig Bay, but Sara didn't mind. Ian was good company and it gave her a chance to regain her cool composure. The light was just beginning to fade as they arrived at a large square house, pleasantly surrounded by tall stands of trees. Substantially built and dignified with age, it was set amidst green lawns overlooking a wide bay. It didn't seem so bleak or isolated as Lochgoil, and its sheltered grounds were colourful with rhododendrons and wide herbaceous borders just coming into bloom.

"It's rather a beautiful old place," Ian murmured appreciatively, as they approached the large front entrance.

"The whole island seems to be here," he whispered later, half under his breath, as he took Sara's arm at the bottom of the winding oak staircase up which she had gone a few minutes ago to leave her wrap.

Near the entrance to the ballroom he introduced her to Mrs Asquith, Beth's widowed mother, and Sir Donald Irvine, Beth's uncle from Glasgow, who was helping with the formalities. Beth was nothing like her mother, Sara decided, as she shook hands with the small motherly-looking woman in front of her. Beth seemed to possess little of her mother's warm friendliness and gentle charm.

After a short while they moved on, Ian introducing her to numerous other people who were gathered in the hall. As he had pointed out, there seemed to be dozens of guests, with many of the men, she noticed, wearing Highland evening dress, and the women long tartan skirts.

In the gaily decorated ballroom a small orchestra played enthusiastically on a slightly raised dais, and in spite of the crowded floor everyone appeared to be joining in and enjoying themselves immensely. The gaiety of the atmosphere was infectious, and within minutes Sara found herself waltzing happily in Ian's arms, with some of her former apprehension fading.

As they danced Ian held her closer and murmured, "You're beautiful, Sara," his lips only inches from her ear, his eyes intent on the ashen sweep of her gleaming hair as he swept her around the floor.

Sara vaguely realized from the deep tone of his voice that one day, as he had already hinted, he might seek more than friendship, and that it might be kinder to find some way of warning him that friendship was all she could ever give. But she was too busy searching over his shoulder for Hugh to give more than perfunctory attention to what he was saying, and most of it went unheeded over her head.

It seemed that at last he guessed that her thoughts were elsewhere, even if he wasn't entirely aware of their direction. "If you're looking for the party from Lochgoil, Sara, I don't think you need worry. They'll be around somewhere, enjoying themselves."

Sara, confused, grasped at the excuse, forcing light laughter. "Actually I was just wondering about Jill," she replied, feeling slightly ashamed of herself. Not that this was so very far from the truth, she thought silently. Jill, and her attendant problems, was never far from her mind!

"I think I caught sight of her before, just as we came in," Ian told her. "Dancing the Gay Gordons. She should be all right. It's some time now since her operation."

Sara smiled, turning back to Ian, glancing up at him as he swung her around, resolving to forget about Hugh. After all, it was Ian who had brought her here this evening, and she owed it to him to be cheerful if nothing else.

Jill was nowhere to be seen, and Sara hoped she wasn't still sulking with Hugh. It seemed a shame that she hadn't been able to bring Colin along—a fact which made her recent behaviour seem all the more foolish. If she had been brave and approached her brother again, Colin might have been here with her having fun.

The waltz drew to a close with an enthusiastic round of applause and Ian whipped her quickly from the floor, his eyes twinkling.

"I'll try to find some refreshments before everyone else gets the same idea," he chuckled. "With this sort of dancing one needs to keep one's strength up."

There were too many people, Sara decided ruefully, as he tried to make way for her. It was almost impossible. "Wherever do they all come from?" she asked, as he managed to find her a quiet spot and a long cool drink.

"You'd be surprised," he replied, smiling as he sat down beside her and looked around. "A lot," he added, "have probably not actually been invited at all. Not that they could be called gate-crashers," he amended hastily. "Usually they're friends of friends, if you know what I mean."

"Yes, I see," she nodded. She supposed, strictly speaking, that she came into this category. She gazed about her, sipping her drink, listening idly to Ian as he pointed out various celebrities who had come over specially for the evening's festivities. She still hadn't seen anything of Jill, but suddenly her nerves tightened as Beth danced past in the arms of an obvious admirer. Tall and dark, she moved with a sinuous grace, her face heavily but beautifully made up. As she passed her eyes fell on Sara, who drew back at the cold hostility in their depths, although in the next minute she felt sure she must have been mistaken. But for a girl about to announce her engagement Beth didn't look particularly cheerful.

Ian, however, allowed her little time to brood, and after supper she was just beginning to feel happier and more relaxed when suddenly Hugh was by her side.

He looked very striking, very elegant as only a tall man could be in evening clothes. Despite other inclinations, she could not deny herself the pleasure of letting her eyes travel over him, the beautiful cut and cloth of his suit, his ruffled shirt, his cuff-links glittering under the light. His eyes sparkled, a silver glitter in his dark sardonic face.

"My dance, I believe." He swept her away before Ian could protest, holding her slightly away from him so that he could see her face.

"Tell me," he said, "do you always give people such a head-to-toe appraisal?"

"I'm sorry. Was I staring? I wondered where you were." The last few words escaped Sara's lips before she could stop them, and she flushed a little, the colour clear under her luminous skin. "I was just admiring your jacket—actually it was Jill I wanted to see."

"In that case, you can stop looking. I've no doubt she's around somewhere, but you'd hardly find a haystack in this crush, my dear, let alone a needle."

"If that's supposed to be funny...!" Perhaps her best way to fight the surge of desire inside her was to antagonize him. "I just wanted a word with her, that's all."

"Won't I do?" he asked suavely. "And please don't spoil my evening by looking scornful. It's something you do very well, especially in the last few days."

He stared at her narrowly, his dark eyes full of speculation as they slipped over her downbent head and the heavy sweep of her lashes. The dress she wore was crêpe georgette, white with deeply cuffed sleeves and a flowing skirt. The bodice fitted closely with a low neckline. It was very soft, very feminine, and in it Sara looked very lovely.

Beneath his intent regard she felt her senses swimming weakly, and her feet stumbled as she felt herself drowning in a sea of despair. Momentarily his arms tightened, pulling her against him; he was not listening to her brief apology, or the neat little excuse which went with it.

Sara fell silent, averting her head, a pulse beating rapidly in her white throat, her blue eyes clouded. She had never experienced anything like this before, and hated him for being the cause of it.

He drew an audible breath as his eyes moved across her face. "Let's get out of here," he said tautly. "This damned crowd, I don't know where Beth gets them."

"It's all for a good cause," Sara protested feebly, as she felt herself propelled firmly through a side door, then along a dark passage towards the back of the house. She wasn't really aware of where she was going.

"I doubt if many of us will ever survive it," Hugh remarked dryly, as he thrust open an outer door and they escaped into the cool fresh air.

Sara found herself walking swiftly along a garden path, through an archway set in an old brick wall, into a shrubbery of tall green firs and a tangle of stunted bushes split by a narrow, scarcely discernible track. Once through this they went down stone steps, unevenly placed, into an alcove beside what appeared to be in the darkness, an overgrown ornamental pool. An old wooden seat, worn smooth by years of weather, stood beside it.

She stared around curiously at the odd patches of garden where the moonlight touched, almost forgetting Hugh for the moment until he said quietly, "No one will find us here."

He paused, a black and white silhouette against the sky, the wind moving shadows across his face as it stirred through the branches of the nearby trees, turning him into a pirate, vividly arrogant and raffish. Sara's heart, which had steadied a little after the race down the path, began to beat again, unevenly.

His smile flickered gently as she looked at him, a white glint in the darkness, but she was faintly surprised when he said, "I used to be friendly with Beth's brother, Ben. He was a racing driver—not that you'll remember him—he was killed a few years ago. This was his special spot. A sort of hideout, he used to call it. We sometimes came here as youngsters to get away from Beth. No one comes here any more, I believe."

"I see. I'm sorry." Tentatively she stood before him, slim in her long white dress, with only her sapphire eardrops to light her pale beauty. "Don't you believe in ghosts?"

"Only the one I'm looking at right now." The smile still played on his lips as he touched an eardrop gently with his finger, so that it moved against her cheek. "Certainly not Ben's. He had too much sense of humour."

Somewhere behind her water still trickled into the neglected pool beneath the growth of weeds. It was the only sound as he stopped speaking, and in spite of a sudden uneasiness, she moved away from him, nearer to the pool and stared down into its dark depth. Tears stung the back of her eyes.

"Ben made that pool himself," Hugh told her, moving to her side, following her glance but missing the tears. "He liked messing around in gardens, building walls, making paths and things like this. I never could reconcile it with his love of speed."

"A garden wouldn't have killed him," she replied, feeling ashamed of the flippant note in her voice, but not daring to let sentiment seep through even slightly. Hugh's own sentimentality seemed just another weapon against the last remnants of her weakening defences. If she wasn't careful even these would crumble away, leaving her totally at his mercy.

She glanced warily at his strong profile, the fine shaping of his lips and firm sculptured jaw. It emphasized the dynamic quality of the man. Yet in his lips and eyes there was also a certain sensitivity, a sympathy for another's pain which she hadn't been aware of before. Suddenly, rather desperately, she wished she was older, or with more experience. He baffled and excited her. He seemed to sense her moods and occasionally set out to put her at ease, but she had no idea how to deal with him. He regarded her with something like amusement, quite capable of ruthlessly storming her guarded heart. Her fingers, groping unconsciously for reassurance, touched the fragile petals of a lilac, and involuntarily she turned, burying her face in the pale, scented flowers.

"Sara!" His laugh was soft, self-mocking, and his voice turned her heart over. He was lifting her high in his arms, carrying her towards the seat. There he put her down and sat by her side, but kept one confining arm around her, his hand curving the fine bone of her shoulder. She stayed with a trance-like immobility as his other hand went to her chin, turning her face up to his, watching the nerve beat in her smooth temple. "You know why I wanted you out here, don't you? Not to talk about Beth or Ben, or Jill. I want to make love to you. Yesterday, on Ben More, you wanted me to. I felt it."

She trembled uncontrollably with revealing shock. "You don't have to feel you owe me anything," she choked, utterly humiliated, her face hot as she tried futilely to pull away from him. How had she come to care so deeply for a man who taunted her so with her own vulnerability?

But she wasn't to escape so easily. The ruthlessness which she had known before was still there, mocking her, hurting her. The momentary tenderness in his hand vanished as the scornful words tripped off her tongue, and he bent her head back towards him, sliding his hands like steel to encircle her narrow waist, his lips hard on her bare nape, holding her prisoner.

There was no pretence about him now, none of the restraint of the night before. Quick darts of fire ran through her body as his lips hurt the soft flesh of her shoulder, caressing the delicate hollows, until she could bear it no longer and turned helplessly in his arms, lifting her own mouth with almost unbearable tension up to his.

A whirlpool of emotion possessed her, swirling away her self-control, destroying all resistance. There was a glimpse of raw little flames in his eyes as he tipped her head back over his arm, and forcibly kissed her. In those few burning seconds she was lost.

The tide of feeling rose between them alarmingly. He was brutal, and then he was indescribably warm and tender, the desire to hurt giving way to the keener pleasure of kissing her eyes, the soft curves of her neck, and her mouth again. Her lips parted against his as she pressed closer to him, and her arms were fast around his broad strong neck.

He could feel her trembling, and he lifted her head as she buried it against his shoulder, forcing her to look at him, noting her small air of desperation, her breathless agitation.

His voice came thickly, "Tomorrow, Sara, you and I are going to talk. Perhaps I shouldn't have brought you out here this evening, but this thing between us is something one can resist for just so long."

The moonlight etched the pure outline of her face. It looked very young and defenceless, her eyes dilated with the violence of her emotions.

"Tomorrow?" Her voice was faint, a thread of sound, scarcely audible, her breath uneven against his lean cheek. She didn't care about tomorrow! There was only tonight and this man who held her in his arms. Desire swept colour under her skin, betraying the flame inside her as it burnt away her last vestige of pride. Now, she had none. She only wanted Hugh to love her as she loved him. Words seemed inadequate, unimportant.

"Darling..." He still held her close, but had control of himself now, his voice steadier with that familiar hint of steel. "You came with McKenzie. I must take you back to him before he seeks us out. You'll tell him you won't go out with him again. Tomorrow will be another day."

Bewildered, Sara drew away from him, her hair spilling over her flushed cheeks, not understanding. Something of her anguish must have transmitted itself as he helped her gently to her feet.

"Sara," his fingers caught her wrist tightly, "I could say something about honour among thieves." He gave a low laugh, entirely without mirth. "I could confess that such a thing has never bothered me before, but this, what we have between us, is something entirely different from anything I've ever known. This has to be exactly right, you know that."

Was he apologizing, or appealing to her better nature? She flung back her head wildly, doubts stinging through her. "What about Beth?" she couldn't stop herself asking, as she stared at him through the darkness. "There's nothing at all between Ian and myself. But you and Beth—Jill said that you would probably announce your engagement this evening."

Her head was swimming, and a tormented feeling welled up inside her. She would have given anything to be able to take back those words. She had been too impulsive. She shouldn't have mentioned Beth, but the impulse to speak had been overpowering.

Momentarily she felt him stiffen, but not, she thought, with anger. With his back to the cloud-covered moon she was unable to see his expression. There was only a faint glitter from his eyes as he said soberly, "Jill talks too much. She always has done—and is good at jumping to the wrong conclusions." He turned on her suddenly and caught her face in his hands. "Don't talk any more, Sara. We'll go back now. As I said before, tomorrow is another day."

The orchestra was playing the last strains of a dance as they reached the ballroom. The bright lights and the gay high spirits of the couples on the floor hit Sara like a discordant note. Her own heavy-heartedness seemed worse since coming from the garden, and Hugh's dark strained face did nothing to dispel her distraught feelings. She felt that she might have dreamt the last hour, that it had never actually existed.

Then the next few minutes seemed to turn the remainder of the evening into a nightmare. In front of their very eyes Jill waltzed gaily towards them in Colin's arms, just as Beth bore determinedly down on them.

A terrible faintness assailed Sara's senses, a totally new, sickening sensation as Beth slipped her hand possessively through Hugh's arm, smiling brightly into his eyes.

"I've been looking for you everywhere, darling." She ignored Sara. "Someone said you were having a drink, but I couldn't find you. I did ask Jill, but she was much too busy enjoying herself with her artist friend from London to be of any help. Of course, I forgave her. She's obviously in love." Her laughter, bright and tinkling, fell like particles of ice on Sara's head.

There was a moment's oppressive silence. The colour began to drain from Sara's cheeks, leaving her pale and frightened-looking. She didn't need to look to see the dark frown gathering on Hugh's face as Jill waved blatantly before she and Colin disappeared again into the crowd.

Beth went on smiling, still holding Hugh's arm, but her eyes were coldly malicious as they studied Sara's slightly dishevelled appearance. It seemed obvious that she was drawing her own conclusions, and not liking what she saw.

Sara realized this when Beth murmured smoothly, "I saw you and Jill going into this artist's holiday cottage yesterday, Sara, but I hadn't time to stop. I was going to ask Jill to bring him along, but fortunately she had the good sense to anticipate the invitation."

Some women, Sara knew, could be diabolically clever when aroused. Beth, she knew, had been aware of Colin's existence and some of the controversy surrounding him. Jill had probably filled in the gaps, even to Sara's own involvement in the matter. Now Beth only needed to twist a few facts while using the same information to suit her own purpose.

Cold crept over Sara's skin, and a feeling of fatality. The thing she had feared most had happened. Hugh knew of her duplicity and the contempt he felt was clearly visible on his face. Through a haze of anguish she heard him say curtly, "If you'll excuse us for a few minutes, Beth, Sara and I will just finish this dance."

Before Sara could protest he swept her away from Beth's disdainful eyes into the throng of dancers. But there was no gratitude in her heart. Now the interrogation would begin. The cynical questions before the final devastating denouncement. Beth seemed quite without scruples. She was in love with Hugh, and it was obvious that she wasn't prepared to share him, that she would make short work of anyone who stood in her way. Well, this time her tactics appeared to have met with unqualified success, and if Hugh's expression was anything to go by she had only a short while to wait before having him back by her side.

Unhappiness began to mount in Sara as panic surged, and her feet stumbled on the smooth floor. Hugh jerked her quickly up against him, his arms hard.

"At least try not to lose your feet along with your integrity," he murmured harshly.

"Please, Hugh," she whispered, desperately trying to keep her voice on an even note, but he cut her off ruthlessly.

"Don't tell me you can explain, that you don't

know what Beth was talking about, because I don't want to hear it."

She stared at him with wide startled eyes, tilting her head back in an effort to see his face. Nothing could be worse than this! Hugh was a stranger, not remotely related to the man who had held her so passionately in his arms in Ben's garden. His eyes raked over her comprehensively, dislike in every taut line of him.

"Please, Hugh," she reiterated, with a shiver of shock, "you must listen, if only for Jill's sake. Couldn't we go somewhere and talk?"

He dismissed her tentative plea out of hand, as she had instinctively known he would. "This will do as well as anywhere else. If we were alone I might resort to physical violence, or even allow you to twist me around your little finger, which you've obviously enjoyed doing in the past."

Who was it who had said that nightmares didn't last? This one could last a lifetime! Stricken, she tried to pull away from him, but he held her in a vice-like grip, his fingers like steel on her narrow waist, and short of making a scene, she could do nothing but follow where he led.

It seemed illogical that in spite of his cynicism she was still consumed by an urgent desire to make him see that she hadn't deliberately set out to deceive him. That she had only acted as she had done out of a conviction that somewhere along the line Colin Brown had been misjudged, and with Gwen at the cottage as a chaperon, it had seemed wiser to give Jill and Colin a chance to sort themselves out, without the incentive of further opposition.

"At least," she said huskily, her hand unconsciously clutching his lapel, "let me tell you that as far as I can see Colin Brown is a very nice young man with a very good job, and is very keen to meet you."

"How very nice!" he mocked. His cool stare hardened, his white teeth snapped together. "No one could say you haven't weighed him up, but spare me the details!"

She wanted to hit out at him frantically, to beat her small clenched fists against him, anything to break that inflexible self-control. "I hate you," she said soberly, from the very depth of her being.

"And heaven help me!" he exploded with soft violence which flicked her as sharply as a knife. A dangerous light flickered through his eyes as they took in her extreme pallor. The crystal chandeliers hanging from the ornate ceiling spilled brilliant light over her face. There was nowhere to hide. Hugh looked like murder, plain unadulterated murder!

"I know all about dear Mr Brown. That is," he amended tersely, "I do now. And as far as I know I can agree with you that he's all right. But that's not the point, and you know it! You deliberately set out to deceive me, and I don't give a damn for extenuating circumstances. I asked something of you, and you agreed, but behind my back you've fought me all along."

Sara's eyes, too big for her white face, met his beseechingly as pain and resentment raced through her veins.

"I don't see it that way, Hugh. I thought I was acting for the best. If I considered my own part at all it came only secondary to my concern for Jill."

Anger washed over his face and his voice was derisive. "Such a neat little speech, Sara. Did you expect an ovation? Instead of protesting so much, why not confess that you were determined to have your own way from the start? Rather like a spoilt child. Well, thanks to Beth, my eyes have been opened, and now I know exactly what you are."

"How dare you!" Hot colour ran wildly over her cheeks, turning her into a small fury. The dance ended with the music crashing in a final crescendo, and they stood staring at each other, regardless of the people around them. Anger stiffened Sara's spine, chasing the tears from her tight throat, and she threw back her head defiantly. "Don't you think," she cried frankly, "that the boot could be on the other foot? You discovered that you were mistaken about Colin Brown, but you didn't think of enlightening anyone else with the information! However did that slip your fabulous memory? Both Jill and I could have been grateful."

Barely coherent, she turned, not waiting for a reply as she almost ran from his side. No great lover of scenes, she was already aware that she and Hugh were attracting some attention. Quickly she made her way out of the ballroom, her heart flooding with relief when almost immediately she bumped into Ian.

He was walking down the hall, obviously looking for her, and she felt a guilty sense of shame as his face lit up as she emerged from the doorway. Was she really as deceitful as she felt? Perhaps. But she found it impossible to fight the emotions which drove her on.

"Please, Ian," she begged, distraught, clutching his arm, her face white, "I've the most dreadful headache. Could you possibly take me home?"

Ian frowned as he looked at her intently, his eyes anxious, his medically trained mind instantly alert. "You haven't had an accident, or anything like that, have you, Sara?"

"Not really ... not unless you could call an argument with one's boss an accident," she replied rather wildly, with a forced laugh. "The dance is nearly over, Ian. I was hoping you wouldn't mind leaving?"

"Oh, of course not." He looked at her a little oddly before glancing at his watch. "Actually I was just going to suggest it myself. In another half hour we'd probably be stuck behind a queue of cars a mile long. If you can manage to find your coat, I'll have the car around to the door in a jiffy."

Sara still felt slightly ashamed when she thought about it a few hours later. It was only after he had left that she realized that he had said very little more. It was almost as if he had inadvertently guessed where her real feelings lay. He had driven her back to Lochgoil without making one adverse comment, although she sensed that he had been curious about her disagreement with Hugh. Well, he would almost certainly find out soon enough—after she had gone.

Her head still ached, in spite of the tablets which he had insisted on her taking, but she tried to ignore it as she jumped out of bed. At least she had had a short, if uneasy, sleep.

It had been the sound of a car in the courtyard below that had woke her up. She remembered that Hugh had arranged to spend the day with John Finley, and would be leaving early. Obviously he wouldn't allow any dispute with his secretary to interfere with his pleasure.

She reached the window just in time to see him disappear, just catching a fleeting glimpse of his dark head as he drove away. As she turned abruptly her eyes fell on her discarded party dress on the floor. In the small hours of that morning, when she had taken it off, it hadn't seemed to matter what happened to it. Nor did it now. In fact there seemed only one thing to do with it. Swiftly she went to the commodious wardrobe and opened the door, reaching for her suitcases and an armful of clothes which she hastily packed.

She must leave Lochgoil straight away. She couldn't bear to stay and face Hugh again, not after the fiasco of the ball. His contempt for her would be too much of an embarrassment between them, apart from her love for him which she might not be able to hide. And there was also a girl's pride. Not, she thought, with a painful jerk of her heart, that she had much of that left—just enough to make her determined to escape. Besides, her work here was nearly done. Hugh shouldn't have any difficulty in completing it himself. Probably Beth would be willing to give him any assistance he might require.

Quickly finishing her packing, Sara made plans. She would ring for a taxi from Salen. The man there was always very obliging. There would be a ferry from Craignure. She didn't know what time, but he would tell her—the island people always knew these things. From Oban she would catch a train to Glasgow, and then London. With any luck she could be home by late evening.

Two hours later she sat on the pier at Craignure. It was only eleven o'clock, but the taxi proprietor had said that the ferry would be there before twelve, so she hadn't long to wait.

The household at Lochgoil had still been sleeping when she left. She had written a short note which she had left in the library for Hugh, and told Biddy briefly that she had been called away. Whether Biddy believed her or not she couldn't be sure, but she had promised to tell the others when they came down. No doubt Hugh would think of a suitable explanation when he returned.

Now, she sat on an overturned fish-crate, just as she had done so many weeks ago when she had first arrived. Only this time she looked towards the sea, rather than the land. And this time it was a boat that she waited for, not a man with a sharp tongue and even sharper eyes, with whom she had formed such a turbulent relationship.

It was a beautiful morning, cool and fresh, with only a faint drift of cloud on the horizon. Sara closed her eyes resolutely against the almost magnetic pull of the scene. Once away from the island she was sure to feel better, but until then she was determined to keep her mind sphinx-like and refuse to think.

Then suddenly her tear-hazed eyes flew open, her heart began pounding, and there was a weakness in her lower limbs. A Land-Rover wheeled off the north road, raced along the pier and drew up with a scream of brakes by her side. A man jumped down, tall and dark . . .

Oh, no! Sara's hand flew to her throat. Not again! Unmindful of the weakness of her legs, she stumbled unsteadily to her feet, blinking her thick lashes, unable to believe the evidence of her own eyes.

This time he didn't stop to ask questions. Without speaking, or even looking at her properly, he picked up her luggage with familiar ruthlessness and flung it haphazardly into the back. Then with the same utter disregard for her feelings he took her forcibly by the arm, and after thrusting her into the passenger seat, jumped in beside her and slammed the door.

"Just where did you think you were going?" he ground out, as he reversed dangerously off the pier.

He was in a furious mood, as she could see, but there wasn't much she could do about it as something seemed to have paralysed her voice. At last she managed, weakly, "You have my note?"

"Yes." He changed gear savagely on a corner. "I certainly have! I've also seen Jill, but that's beside the point. Jill has no brains, but I expected more of you."

His extreme sarcasm was not lost on her. She turned very quickly and stared out of the window, tears stinging the back of her eyes. "I thought you'd gone for the whole day," she murmured inaudibly.

His jaw clamped tight. "And so you were running home to Jane, and London," he said tersely.

There was a long silence. The palms of Sara's hands were moist and she clenched her fingers around them tightly. The Land-Rover sped on. The road narrowed, and suddenly he whipped the vehicle up a side-track and stopped. They were surrounded by tall pine trees. She recognized the place immediately. It was where they had stopped before, on that first day.

Hugh switched off the engine and rounded on her at once, his eyes grimly noting her startled expression. "Now," he said sharply, unmercifully, "we're going to talk, you and I."

Something was aching at the base of Sara's throat and she pressed her hand to it instinctively. "Well, do so by all means, if you think it will make any difference," she forced herself to say carelessly.

His hand shot out to her shoulder, deliberately hurting, gripping it hard. "Just listen!" The dark eyes glinted sardonically, and the inflection in his voice brought a flush to her cheeks.

"I'd arranged to spend the day with John Finley, but after what happened last night I changed my mind. Unfortunately he's not on the phone, so there was no other way but to drive over and explain. Mistakenly, I expected you all to be still in bed when I got back."

His dark eyes held hers until she could stand it no longer. Her eyelids dropped. "You said you've seen Jill?" she whispered.

"Yes," he bit off curtly, "and she's explained a lot. All about bullying you to go along with her plans to keep her boy-friend hidden. I'm afraid she was quite furious when I told her it hadn't been necessary."

As he paused reflectively Sara said urgently, "You said something about Colin at the dance. Something about him being all right?"

He put a finger under her chin, making her look at him again. "Colin Brown had been caught in a drugs raid, in a big city club. I don't suppose Jill thought to mention that!"

As Sara shook her startled head he went on, "Fortunately he was cleared, but before this happened Jill's mother received disturbing news about her first husband in America. You see, she'd been a widow for five years before she married my father, and if the information she had received was correct it could have meant that her first husband was still alive, and I suppose, technically speaking, that she'd never been legally married to my father at all. And all this on top of my father's death! The poor woman was nearly out of her mind.

"However, it has proved to be a case of mistaken identity. To cut a long story short, her first husband was lost in a bad air crash over Mexico, and his papers had fallen into another chap's hands. Then after all this time this same man is involved in a serious accident, and these papers are found on him. They were the only means of identification the police had, and this is why they contacted London."

Dismayed, Sara tried to sort it out. "Couldn't Jill have gone with her—or you, perhaps?"

"She refused to consider this. Of course her sister in Baltimore is with her, but she doesn't want Jill to know anything about it, especially now that there's no need. Rumours have an insidious way of getting around."

"And so she asked you to keep an eye on Jill while she was away, and you more or less ordered my co-operation as soon as I arrived . . ."

His mouth was mocking and tender. "Remember, Sara, the domestic scene wasn't mine, not then, at any rate. Maybe I did overplay it a bit. A heavy-handed defence against a pair of beautiful blue eyes."

She tried to retain a degree of sanity and to ignore her racing heart. "Last night, you said you knew that Colin was all right, yet you never mentioned this before."

He grimaced wryly. "Because I didn't think it necessary. I actually thought that Jill had forgotten about him. Put it down, if you like, to my state of mind!"

"But when did you find out?" Sara persisted.

"When I went down to London and saw James Kerr. He was looking into the case for me. This was when," his eyes softened, "I met Jane Marlee, and we talked."

The breeze through the open window stirred Sara's hair. She refused to be sidetracked. "Last night you were so furious!"

"Of course, my darling," his tone was light, purposely mocking. "You might recall that I wasn't aware that Mr Brown was on the island, let alone firmly established in a cottage, and when Beth murmured the information so sweetly in my ear I'm afraid I saw red. Not particularly about his being here—it was your knowing about it which rocked me."

Her eyes were wide, deeply shadowed. She looked

back at him, her soft curved lips parting with contrition.

"I am sorry, Hugh. Please believe me."

"Darling," he caught her close, feeling with fierce satisfaction her slender yielding body against his own. "I'm the one who must apologize, not you. I can only say that love can make a man sensitive as well as blind. Last night I wanted to beg you to marry me. Heaven knows, I've never let anything stand in my way before. It was something crazily mixed up with Ben and Ian MacKenzie that stopped me. I wanted the setting right, perhaps because I'd never proposed to a girl before. Normally Beth's sweet vindictiveness doesn't bother me."

"You don't love her?" Contrarily, and very femininely, Sara's arms went up around his neck.

Hugh leaned down to her. "There's never been anything between Beth and me, darling. She only thinks she likes me more than other men."

She smiled gently but didn't argue. Somehow Beth Asquith didn't matter any more.

His lips were against hers with gently deepening pressure, and there was nothing humble about him now. He was all demanding male as his arms crushed her to him.

"I love you," he said, in a low swift voice. The moan of the wind was the only sound for some minutes, until he lifted his dark head and stared down at her softly flushed face. "I love you, darling," he repeated thickly, "but would you be prepared to marry me and live at Lochgoil? I intended running the estate and keeping an eye on the London office from here."

From the whirlpool of emotions surrounding her she raised starry eyes to his, her mouth quivering.

"I'll look after you, Sara," he promised. "I'll try to make up for all you've lost."

From somewhere out in the woods a bird was singing, and the air was filled with the green summer fragrance of the island. There was a tenderness in his voice which she couldn't deny.

"Darling," she murmured indistinctly, "I love you so much that I wouldn't mind where we lived, but Lochgoil would be perfect. Lochgoil, and the two of us together," she whispered, as his lips came down on hers once more.

She had come here such a short time ago with an aching heart. Now it was thundering in tune with the man who held her so tenderly, and there was nothing in her heart but the sound of the sea, and music.